MISSISSAUGA YOUTH ANTHOLOGY

VOLUME VI

INK MOVEMENT

MISSISSAUGA YOUTH ANTHOLOGY
VOLUME VI

Compiled by:
Rana Al-Fayez

Editors:
Emi Roni, Aleeza Qayyum, Seerat Rehman, Catherine Hu,
and Sally Co

Cover Design:
Cecilia Tsang, Sally Co

Inside Design:
S.B. Aguinaldo

Published by:
In Our Words Inc. /inourwords.ca / inourwords2008@gmail.com
251 Queen Street South, Suite #561, Streetsville, ON L5M 1L7

ISBN: 978-1-926926-92-6

Dear Reader,

Thank you for picking up a copy of Volume VI of the Mississauga Youth Anthology, an initiative of Ink Movement Mississauga.

Over the past few months, this Anthology volume has been Ink Movement's baby. Our entire team has carefully read, edited, and compiled over 150 pieces of artwork, photography, poetry, and prose submitted by youth from across the Peel Region and beyond—this is more content than we have ever received before! I believe that every single piece submitted is truly a testament to the vitality of the artistic spirit within the Peel Region. Furthermore, I am amazed by the sheer poignancy of the topics shared—the stories featured within the pages of this anthology are proof of the power young people possess to empower one another and create social change.

To continue the baby metaphor, it takes a village to raise a child, and it also takes an army of team members, community partners, and mentors to publish an anthology. As a result, there are many individuals and organizations to thank.

To Maxwell Tran, who founded Ink Movement six years ago—thank you for bringing Ink Movement into the world and for trusting us with the continuation of your legacy. We hope that you are aware of the immense respect the entire Ink Movement team has for you and everything you have done to further the arts in Mississauga.

To Cheryl Antao-Xavier who owns our publishing company In Our Words Inc.—thank you so much for always taking the time out of your day to sit down with us to proofread the Anthology and for connecting us to your extensive network of authors and artists.

To Jessica, Sharada, Sadaf, and everyone at the Art Gallery of Mississauga—thank you for being such a supportive partner organization and being so generous with your resources and time.

To Andrew and the entire Mississauga Arts and Culture Grant Selection Committee, as well as the Ministry of Education—thank you so much for your generous financial support and for believing in Ink Movement and the power of art in Mississauga.

To Rana, Catherine, Aleeza, Emi, Cecilia, Seerat and Sally—thank you for all the time and love you have put into this Anthology. And of course, to Amna—thank you for all the late-night calls, for putting up with the team's crazy schedule, and for always teaching me how to properly format documents. I cannot think of a more lovely and supportive group of people to be surrounded by over the course of the last few months.

Finally, to you, the reader—we have sent the Anthology out into the world in the hope that it will reach and inspire others as much as we have been inspired by the amazing content within these pages. We hope you enjoy reading it as much as we enjoyed creating it.

With love,

Sonya Zhang

President,
Ink Movement Mississauga

Dear Reader,

We all have something in common; we all have stories to tell.

Love, loss, hope, suffering, elation or despair—this anthology carries our youth's stories through poetry, prose, art and photography. This year we received a record-breaking number of submissions from talented storytellers all over Mississauga.

Sometimes it is hard to open up, to have a conversation, to confront ourselves or others. Sometimes it is easier to express ourselves with a pen, a few brushstrokes, or perhaps a digital eye. Creative self-expression allows us to unearth hidden passion and follow our inspiration. When I look at this year's submissions, I realize that I have learnt so much about the people around me that I wouldn't have known otherwise. I discovered aspects of their characters that I didn't know existed—I was able to acknowledge that I can be short-sighted. I appreciate the perspectives that I was allowed to see.

What's beautiful is that these pieces of work are timeless. I habitually revisit previous year's anthologies, and this anthology is going to be another one added to my collection. This anthology is a celebration of the talent and diverse voices of youth in Mississauga. Ultimately, this is our goal—to allow people to creatively express themselves, using art to create change, whether that be social reformation or personal development.

I would also like to thank and congratulate everyone who took part in this initiative. To the artists and the Ink family—your effort and dedication in compiling this anthology is truly remarkable. I hope you all gained from this journey as much as I did (or more!). I would have loved to name each and every one of you but I have a word limit to my foreword—so together with Sonya's message, I hope we express our deep appreciation for your valuable contribution to this anthology.

So my friend, grab your go-to beverage, sit back and enjoy the read. What you're holding in your hands are documented pieces of people's lives.

Here's to starting conversations.

Stay *ink*spired,

Amna Zia

Vice-President, Ink Movement Mississauga

Dear Reader,

Thank you for picking up a copy of *The Mississauga Youth Anthology: Volume VI*, and for embarking with us on this wild journey. Of course, I'm biased, but I truly believe that this year's Anthology is the most incredible, spectacular, diverse and amazing one yet.

Under the theme "Dear World," the submissions we received covered a wide range of art forms, ideas, topics and styles. Many were impassioned reflections on people, places, events and culture; others were an animated call for justice and unity in our divided world. All were deeply personal, a microcosm of the emotions, passions and talent of youth in our community today. As you flip through the writing, artwork and photography in the pages before you, I hope you feel as inkspired and hopeful as I do.

To all the talented local youth who have contributed to this publication— thank you for sharing your stories in this book. You are extraordinary artists, and it has been a great honour and privilege to showcase your talent to the world.

To my wonderful and lovely team of editors and graphic designers— thank you for your tireless dedication and enthusiasm in carrying this project through to completion.

And to you, dear reader—thank you for picking up a copy of this remarkable book and giving the stories enclosed a home. It is one thing to have the opportunity to tell your story, it is quite another to be heard. Without your excellent taste in reading material, our message would be lost.

Enjoy.
Much Love,

Rana Al-Fayez

Mississauga Youth Anthology Project Lead,
Ink Movement Mississauga

Since Ink Movement was born in 2012, our focus has been helping young people share their stories with the world. These are stories that are often not told in mainstream literature. We wholeheartedly believe that young people matter, and that their voices deserve an audience.

This year, we are putting our philosophy in explicit terms with the theme "Dear World." We asked young writers, artists, and photographers: *What is the message that you want to share with the world?*

As you might expect, the responses varied widely. We received submissions about love, struggle, social issues, and everything in between. We purposely chose a broad theme because we wanted to celebrate the diversity of ideas, passions, and lived experience of young people in our city.

Flip through these pages and you may find yourself surprised by the candor, the bravery, and the creativity of our young artists, many of whom are still in high school. If I can request a favour of you, say their names out loud. Share your favourite pieces with a friend. Acknowledge them on social media. If we want to truly reach the world, it starts with each person who picks up this book.

Thank you in advance, and I hope that you enjoy Volume VI of the Mississauga Youth Anthology.

Happy Reading,

Maxwell Tran

Founder and Executive Director, Ink Movement

Table of Contents

dear world

PLEASE BE ADVISED, THIS ANTHOLOGY CONTAINS STORIES OF YOUTHS' EXPERIENCES WITH SEXUAL ASSAULT, RACISM, DISCRIMINATION, AND MORE.

NOOR B. TOEAMA

My Love Letter To The World

A brief description of humanity's history of mistreating the Earth. A reflection on the feelings and thoughts associated with our beautiful planet. A resolution to take environmental action and care for our home. A love letter to the World.

Dear World,

I miss you. I remember the first time I opened my eyes and caught a glimpse of your beauty. My heart felt as if it was beating faster than the speed of light and I was blown away by your many wonders—I could not believe that I could call *you* my home. I just wanted to thank you for all the invaluable gifts that you've given me. I don't know how I can ever repay all those years of love and happiness that you have blessed me with—since the day I was born.

I know we don't see each other as much as we used to, and I'm sorry—that's my fault. It's painfully not the same as it was, like when we were younger; life's just gotten in the way of our connection. But, you understand, right? Either way, I will always regret the way we ended things. Often I stare out through the window while at school or work and wonder about you; how you are, if you're being treated well, what we could've been, if you miss me too... I wish I can just escape out of this cruel reality and be with you again.

I keep promising myself that I will put in more effort to visit you—but often, you seem *so* far away, although I know that you're always here. Time and time again I've mistreated you, abused you, ignored you; I've been a monster, I've been insensitive. It's not that I don't care about you or want to harm you, it's just that I often forget how valuable and irreplaceable you are. Our downfall came due to the way that I neglected our relationship—I wasn't taking enough precautions to attend to your needs. However, I finally understand that you're not some tool that I can simply use then get rid of. No, you're much more than that. In fact, you are all that matters and I'm so sorry it's taken me this long to realize your true worth. But I see my mistakes now and I want to do better. I have evolved and grown, please give me a chance to prove to you that I am ready to make a change.

I know we have a painful past—if only I was able to take back all that's happened between us and return to those sweet times when everything felt so natural. But I can't, and that's stressful. After years of reflecting on all of the ways that I was destructive towards you, I have developed many methods and devices that will aid me to clean up the mess I've made. I know I left you hurt and suffering, but I'm here now. Allow me to begin a healthy relationship with you, and I promise that I will never let you down again. You will become my top priority and I will cherish over anything else; money, reputation, politics—none of these matter to me as much as you do.

World, I love you. I hope that you'll take me back. This year is the year to genuinely take action; I feel prepared and excited to start over. I know it will be hard at first to adjust and quit all of my old bad habits, but looking forward, I can see us sharing a beautiful future. I'm willing to put in more energy and time than ever before to ensure that we get on good terms.

You *are* and will *forever* be my home, please take me back.

Yours Truly,

Noor Toeama

PUJITA VERMA

When it Rains (Dear World)

I am convinced that your raindrops are tears forming
Lakes in clouds and once they reach a tipping point
They spill over and drizzle as a reminder that
Everything is temporary

Maybe clouds are impatient, marking
Temper with an overcast grey
My neighbours know when to put away their lawn chairs
Though I am unfamiliar with the conventional cues

I still leave open my windows in pouring weather
(Sometimes because I am forgetful)
Most times because I feel like closing the windows is like
Turning my back when you are at your weakest

We eagerly indulge in sunlight but quickly shut the curtains
A foggy kind of flawed logic
Too foggy to remember when rainfall was a privilege
And we would dance in ethereal showers

The drizzle tears from the brimming clouds
That spilled over start advancing in intensity
Suddenly it is a storm worthy of a region-wide weather alert
Too unsafe to leave windows open

A marching band plays on our rooftops the
Steady drum to resonate and set the background rhythm
So we sing along to the makeshift music
Waiting for the skies to clear

HEBA ALFAYEZ

Hard Water Makes for Strong Minds

MELISSA REZK

My People

'My People' is a poem illustrating the strength of the Coptic Christians in Egypt, emphasizing how brutally treated the Copts are. Still, the faith of the Coptic nation can never be shaken.

"Your people, they're dead"
    Sure enough, the news was on the screen, and as I saw,
    A few more were killed while I was standing there in awe.
    "We're very sorry for your loss," as their arms were widespread,
    I backed away politely, "Do not be sorry," I said.
    "Your people, they're dead"
    Do not pity me and apologize for what you think is 'my loss,'
    Understand my people's story; why my people are the nation of
        the cross.
    Grasp why my people die, and question why my people's families
        rejoice,
    Attempt to fathom my people's acceptance of torture, not by
        consequence, but by choice.
    "Your people, they're dead"
    My people became engulfed with sounds of gunfire, and throat-
        scratching screams,
    It had become the ordinary to see shattered buildings from
        explosive machines.
    My people watch streams of blood flow away from wounds
        unhealed,
    Still, my people's word inspires, and my people's faith remains
        concealed.
    "Your people, they're dead"
    My people face the cries of fire; hearing the cracks of broken
        crystal.
    Eyes fall under the screams of shame, while held to my people's
        skull, the eye of a pistol.
    Dignity is taken, as my people try to inhale the breath the
        massacre stole,

Heads drop to the dirt and on the news my people are added to
the death toll.
"Your people, they're dead"
Each precious life murdered that had created the gruesome
scene,
Was merely devalued to a number; 21, appearing on your
television screen.
Now tell me why the stories of my people's faith in despair,
Come from a suited news anchor, relaxing on a $300 chair?
"Your people, they're dead"
Why is it that the white man claims to fully comprehend?
The lives of my people, and why each one comes to an end?
Like a bird attempting to explain why the fish swims at sea,
While the sounds of obliteration scream my people's reality.
"Your people, they're dead"
My people revisit the collapsed structures where red stains the
concrete,
Unceasingly returning, despite the blood of martyrs drowning
their feet.
As swords congregate at my people's necks, my people's heads
tilt higher.
The executioners see weakness, but it's my people's strength
they've yet to acquire.
"Your people, they're dead"
Persecutors tried to bury my people, but little did they know
that my people were a seed,
Pushing them further into the ground is the only way my people
would be freed.
Blood replaces water, as bodies collapse to the ground,
Yet, seconds later, my people rise up; heads held up with a
crown.
"Your people, they're dead"
Do you know why my people look up, not down, as their hands
are tied with rope?
For this is not a symbol of shame—to my people, it signifies
hope.
Have you not realized when my people die black is not worn, it's
white?

My people's tears are not ones of sorrow, but simply ones of
    delight.
"Your people, they're dead"
Wooden crosses are left in the bend of each neck and held
    within cut hands,
Yet, my peoples' faces show a peace this world could never
    understand.
Martyrdom cannot end anything, this is only just to begin.
Even with these millions killed, my people are the ones who still
    win.
"Your people, they're dead"
The world's ears can be deaf to my people and the world's vision
    can be blurred,
But one day the world will take my people's burning and make it
    into words.
Lives can be stolen, yet this only means the earthly flesh will be
    gone.
But, when the soul departs, it leaves this world, and true life will
    live on.
"Your people, they're dead"
Sure enough, the news was on the screen, and as I saw,
A few more were killed while I was standing there in awe.
What loss is this, if it's eternity my people have gained?
"You must be familiar with my people, the Coptic people," I
    exclaimed.
I told them they were mistaken with their apology, "Do not be
    sorry" I said,
"Yes, my people did die, but no, my people are not dead."

KEEVA SZETO

In Places That Feel Like Home

It is a common misconception that you must travel far and chase after that special something to tell a good story. But, the best stories start where the journey starts—home. It isn't just a place, but something that we carry with us, no matter where we are. It is the reminiscence of home that shapes our stories and makes them different from anyone else's.

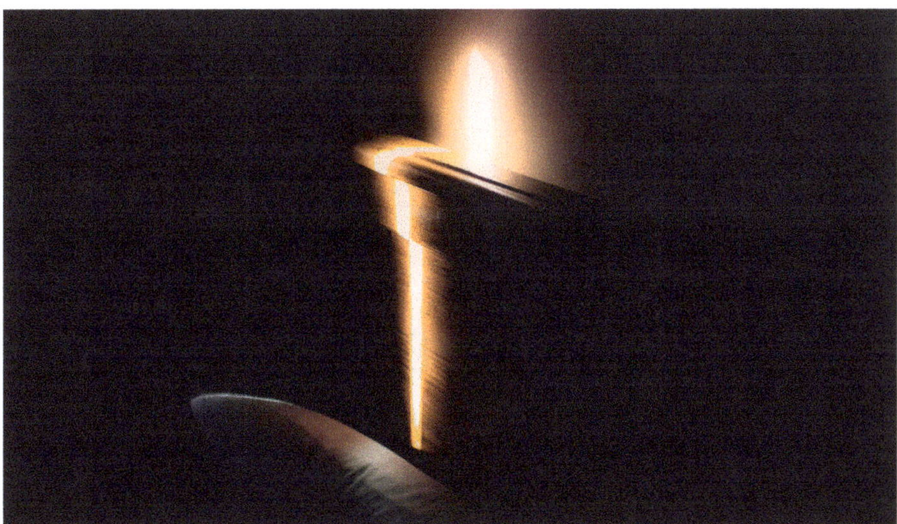

DANIELLA SERRADOR

"A Proposition"

The tough lover's lament
I am not sweet
But I am kind.
There is little in me that is soft and pretty,
Little that is gentle,
Not a shade of milky white in my complexion
For it's red,
All my femininity seeping from the blood
That grows and leaves me in cycles of moon.

There is little sugar in me,
And so I never taste saccharide.
My skin shall never muddle your palate white falsities.
For though I lack servicing lips,
I lack too a tongue that lies.
No silver but flesh.

There is little in me that is soft and pretty because the strong
    just would not tolerate it,
Won the fight to push them out just as the fire forged my spirit.
Honour won the right to govern my being.

I lack pity but am full of empathy.
I am not easy, but perhaps worthwhile.
I am so very full of love,
But of the painful,
Fiercest,
Kind.
The kind that hurts.
The kind that grows.
The kind that builds.

I am not sweet, but I am kind.
Please, please, please.
Let me try.

FIONA YANG

Dreamer

RIANNA ALARAKHIA

That Number on the Page

Dear World, here is what goes on inside my head when I hear students around me crying, stressing, and harassing themselves about their grades. No number can define someone who is honest, trustworthy, and intelligent in their own unique way. Saying you hate yourself because of one test that said "50%" will never stop you from achieving your dreams.

Why does it matter?
Those numbers on the paper
Do not define you

Why ever listen
When you're told you're a failure?
Believe in yourself

It's not what you do
It's what goes on in your head
It's all different

They are far too low
It's not just one's perspective
It is the whole world's

When she looks at you
The way you look at yourself
Makes all the difference

Dare to Dream

The artwork "Dare to Dream Big" portrays how you shouldn't be afraid to dream big, because it will reshape your perspective in life and will benefit you to alter your way of thinking: to push you forward rather than holding you back. No matter how many obstacles or barriers there are: you shouldn't give up on hope, because it could cause you to miss out on success. Setting a goal, and chasing your dream is one step towards becoming successful.

ANONYMOUS

I Never Thought It Could Happen to Me… But It Did

"It won't happen to *me*." It's what we subconsciously tell ourselves when we hear of the harrowing, unimaginable monstrosities unfolding all around the world. Whether by optimism, naiveté or sheer ignorance, I fell prey to this mindless way of thinking. I never thought it could happen to me... until it did.

In late January 2017 I was sexually assaulted. No words can express the gut-wrenching feeling of horror, disgust, emptiness and fear that I felt when I awoke to my naked, vulnerable body being demeaned, objectified and unwillingly explored. My senses were heightened to the point where I could feel every one of his unwelcome touches and every heartrending movement of his tongue. My mind was panicking, my heart was pounding, but my body was paralyzed in shock and terror. It's better to submit to him rather than pathetically and unsuccessfully fight back, right? He was nearly double my weight and triple my strength. No one else was home. No one would hear my cries. There was no way out. I kept my eyes shut tight and the rest of the night blurred by. I quickly grew numb to everything. I felt as though my mind had left my body and I, to this day, can't recall how or when the assault ended.

It's funny how we unreasonably blame ourselves for things that are obviously not our faults. I didn't want to be sexually assaulted. I never asked for it. I never gave consent. Yet, I couldn't shake the overwhelming feelings of embarrassment and guilt. I was so stupid to trust him. It was my fault for letting him stay over. Boys will be boys. I should have known better. If I had fought back, things would've been different. I'm such a coward. I'm so powerless. What's the point in living if I have no control over my life?

For eight months I stayed quiet about my experience. Alone, I suffered from crippling panic attacks in the school bathroom stalls. Alone, I crumbled under his disdainful, smug stare from across the cafeteria. Alone, I spent countless nights uncontrollably bawling until I crashed from complete exhaustion. Alone, I contemplated if it was worth living if I would continue to feel like this for the rest of my life. Everything reminded me of him: the school hallways, the cafeteria, the classroom, the movie theater, the gym, and worst of all, my own bed.

Closure. I needed closure. I needed to know why he did what he did, I needed to know that he knew that what he did was wrong, and above all, I just needed a sincere apology. Then I could move on, or so I hoped. It took an insane amount of courage to confront him, but I thought the end result would be worth it. Unfortunately, I was wrong. He outright denied that he had done anything culpable. "It was obvious you wanted to have sex with me," "You were basically asking for it," "No one's going to believe you." Looking back now, I see the pathetic cowardice and falsity in his statements, but in that moment, when I was already so hopeless and lost, his lies seemed like truths. I grew scared to share my story, in fear that I would be called a liar, a drama queen, an attention-seeker and a whore.

Finally, I decided that enough was enough. I couldn't go through this alone and I needed help. I slowly reached out to friends, family, teachers, therapists and social workers. I'm not going to lie, it didn't get better right away. In fact, it got worse. In order to share my story, I had to revisit that horrendous night that I had tried so hard to forget. I had to let myself feel those raw, heart-wrenching emotions that I had been suppressing for so long.

Eventually, things actually started to get better. The healing process has been long, and I'm still not fully recovered, but I feel so much better than I did before. I'm no longer ashamed of what happened because it truly was not my fault. I'm a sexual assault victim, but that doesn't make me weak nor powerless. I'm strong for choosing to live when it was easier to die, and I'm courageous for fighting to regain my confidence and self-worth.

SEREEN AZIZ

Souk Al-Hamidyah

KIROLLOS KILADA

Do Not Disturb

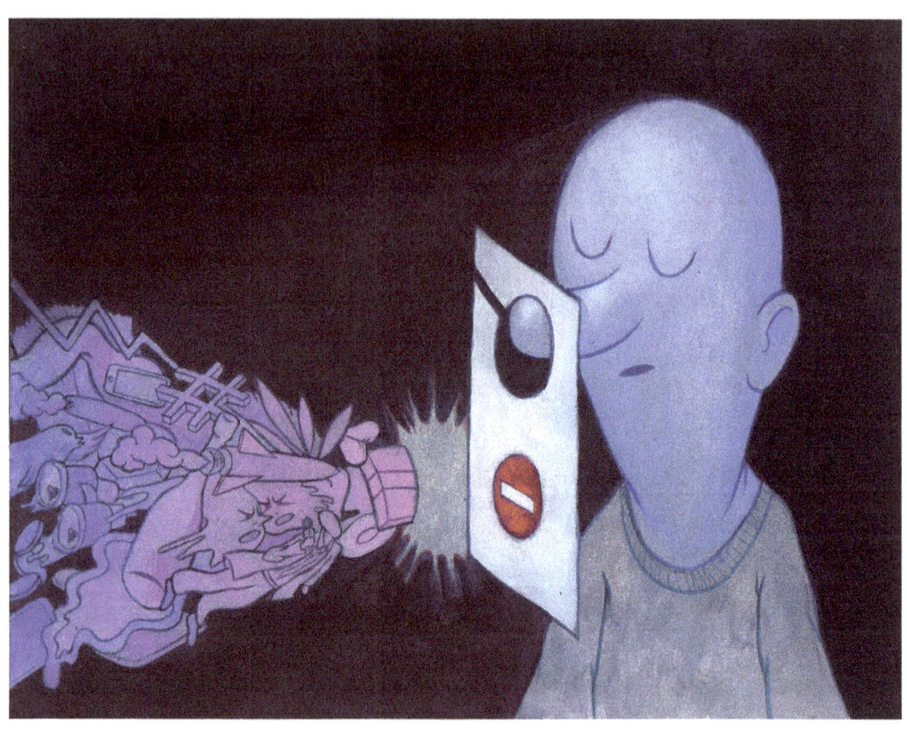

SELENA ZHOU

We, the people

our skin colour is not white,
it is the faintest blue in the foreign winds
our skin colour is not yellow,
we are the delicious baby pink of a newborn
our skin colour is not black,
watercolour merely stained the soles of our feet
our skin colour is not brown,
because it is so much more.

my skin is the colour of peach seeds,
the ripe flesh of a strawberry.
my skin is the colour of the new cloud in a clear sky,
my skin was meant to glow,
my skin was meant to fly.
a people cannot be defined by one colour,
you cannot say that there is only black in Africa,
for I have seen so much more.
I have seen the swirls of purple and pink,
and there are hidden pockets of orange in their dimples.
you cannot say there is only red and yellow in Asia,
we have the slightest touch of evergreen,
and smallest hint of quiet sky blue,
more hues than you could admit to.
you cannot say that there is only white in America,
we have so many diverse colours and shades.
because different shades are different colours,
and our colours fit on every spectrum of the wheel.

but when you give one colour to one people,
you deprive them of their diversity.
you give privilege to lighter shades and denounce darker,
even though they are all so beautiful,
the same beauty but shown in different ways.
please don't slap black and white on everything and call that
    diversity!
you are missing all the other colours of the rainbow.

I am proud of my skin because it is one of the chapters in my
    book.
my skin is not my definition, but it is a part of it,
and that chapter is different in everybody's definition.

yes, there have been times when I have learned to be
uncomfortable in this skin that adds a different bit to me.
not by choice but by circumstance,
we deserve to feel just as beautiful as we really are.
my skin colour is not yellow.
my skin colour is a creamy buttercup in sunshine glow.

so when the night sky clears and the moon borrows light,
remember that we are more than just black or white.
our cameras have developed enough to capture every different
    pixel
it can capture every colour of the rainbow
because that is who we are
we, the people.

ALI MALIK

Cultural Sensitivity, Series One

Series one signifies a deep heritage throwback to South Asian traditional use of clay pottery. The authenticity of the designs and set-up inspired a series of photographs wanting to reflect all the beautiful practices in cultures.

AMIRA BOUCHEMA

Nurse

It's all muffled
But I can still hear it
The cries, the sirens
Wailing into my half-submerged ears
I'm numb from everything
The pain became my sedative
I can feel your tears flow down my face
As your forehead is against mine
But I can't say a word
But these 8
As the blood burns my throat
I try to shrug a smile
Hoping it'll be alright
"I need you like I need a nurse"

Day 1,
I hear you screaming over the sound
And I'm hoping it doesn't sound like a Pierce the Veil song
Your blue gown is nothing but red and black
And I hear you say the diagnosis
Of "overdose of amentia, suicide and psychosis,"
But I can only smile at the thought
Because my love was schizophrenic
And you were its happy blue pills
The monitor clipped in my arm
And through my swollen virgin veins
My vision then becomes like a Picasso painting
And you're starting to look like the man from Scream
"I need you like I need a nurse"

Day 10,
Discharged for barely 10 minutes
And people I have endangered as I live
As I laid my body on the empty road
Waiting for it,
And they used to dare call us Generation Unafraid
But it's hard to believe that you don't fit the picture
And as I meet you again
Lips locked in mine,
Tasting sweet like morphine and codeine
And my bruised soiled veins by heroin
Can't help but grasp your wrist to the snapping point
But you are breathing me back to life
"I need you like I need a nurse"

Day 11,
You then look like a witch,
Making me float to the operation room
Words of bitterness,
I can hear your soul crack into pieces
And you can't seem to hold on but I can't help but question
Why you are still with me
I only brought you trouble since the day you met me
If I was you by now I would have away
Somehow instead you forgave me
You say you have to do what has to be done
Even if it means you deny yourself the truth
But you can't seem to understand
That life's but a walking shadow
A poor player
That struts and frets his hour upon the stage
"I need you like I need a nurse,"

Day 20,
This is the end; my final lines are coming through
But somehow you always seem to find me
Upon the edge of a bridge

I have become schizophrenic
Bipolar
Psychotic
Narcoleptic
"Find the nearest ledge" you say
"Walk out" they say
Suspend you say
Wouldn't the world be a better place without me?
Like the vivid nightshade
Yesterday I said, that you my nurse wouldn't catch me
With a needle in hand,
To induce numbness in me
And you wait for one last breath from me
"I need you like I need a nurse"
I need you like I need a nurse,
to repair my head and my feelings that don't hold up well
        anymore
to replenish my stock of serotonin, to tell me that it's nothing.
I need you like I need a nurse
To come huddle me in your arms,
I'm bad luck and you should know that
I want you to be happy and not poisoned
By my life
Because my blood is black from my sins
But I still dearly hope that
someway, somehow
Your gown will go back to blue
Your words won't mutter any diagnosis
Or your hands won't hold any needles
Your lips will not taste like morphine and codeine
Or will your tears flow down my face
This time,
You'll be back to the way you used to be
I'll jump off that ledge
And you won't be wasting your breath
To resuscitate a deadman.

JUSTINA YANG

Breathe

Dear World...life is full of beauty. Notice it. Take time time to have a moment to just stop. breathe. appreciate. You owe yourself that much.

KENISHA ARORA

Barbie Doll

Barbie Doll is a poem that describes this mentality that many have of girl. A mentality that implies that girls must be the ideal image and must behave like a delicate lotus. How many girls are expected to be a certain person, Barbie. This poem was written to help the audience be more aware of the perspective of a female. By using the word "must" repetitively it shows the devastation and insecurity that these girls are going through because they have to live under certain expectations.

I must wear makeup and have flawless skin
Spidery long legs,
And you must've known where I have been

My hair must be chic without a bobby pin,
Perfect as a picture
I must wear makeup and have flawless skin

I must be Barbie's twin,
Act like I fit in
And you must've known where I have been

I must have a high chin
Be confident and sanguine
I must wear makeup and have flawless skin

I must be pure but not within
Must look like the diamond in the magazine
And you must've known where I have been

My roar must be like a mandolin
Thoughts and dreams hard to contain
I must wear makeup and have flawless skin
And you must've known where I have been

SHOFFANA SUNDARAMOORTHY

Snowy Nights

Walking through Seattle,
Hands buried in my pockets
As I make my way through
The streets accompanied with
Jack's frostbite and his friends,

The snowflakes as they danced
And twirled around me.

They looked so wondrous
For it complemented
The starless, night sky.
How they floated along
So effortlessly, together.

I finally arrived to that house
That I called home for so long,
But haven't came back to
In way too long.

All the quarrels, all the tears,
And yet it somehow worked for
At least this long, perhaps
It was because I finally left,
Moved out to become my own.

It couldn't be.

It took forever to shed the wool
That was made out of myself
Being the family's black sheep.

I slowly make my way to the porch.
A smile beams as I notice how father
Finally set up those Christmas lights.
Back then, it was the same.
Father would try with all his might,
Only to mess up, cuss out the family
Before heading off to the bar, and
Arriving back in his jolly, drunk daze.

I climb the steps, gripping the railing
Reminiscing about my younger days,
Shorter stature.
My brothers and sisters would
Never let me live that down.

I reach the door,
But before I knock,
I hear laughter.
I sense happiness.

I make my way to the window,
Passing by mom's old chair,
To peer inside, past the curtains.

There's everyone.
They looked happy,
Happier than I have ever seen,
Happier than I have ever witnessed.

The realization of my reality...
I take one last look through the
Window, and there goes a sigh.

I get up and make my way
From this place that holds
In this beating heart of mine.

I realized that as long as the memory of me
Still lingered and stenched up those walls,
They truly could never have been happy.

I should have seen this coming,
The way they never invited me
To family events, or how they
Would never return my calls.

How delusional.

I take one last look,
At that house, before
Heading back onto the road.

I wished Jack brought
His snowflakes back,
So that I wouldn't be
Like this on a new year,
All alone.

ADRIANO BROWN

What Makes a Community

A small digital collage of some of the members in Mississauga's community worth appreciating.

KHYATHI RAO

Home

The mirror in our house had seen everything,
From the day my little sister was born,
To the day my brother was called off to war.

It had seen our laughs, tears, fights and mourning.

Placed on the mantelpiece, like it had been for six years,
It was there, yet not there.
Nobody paid much attention to it,
Until our house was bombed by the enemy.

Our house, which preserved memories,
Of my first tooth falling off,
Memories of the time I got punished by mama.
It was no more...

Memories of the warm, cozy bear hugs that my dad gave.
In a fraction of a second, all was lost...*all*.

My very own parents joined the countless stars in the sky,
Leaving me, with my sister and a half-burnt mirror,
That somehow survived the fire.

We are rescued from the rubble,
Given a place to sleep and eat, along with other kids,
Until we were sent off to some country, as refugees.
Only if someone could do the same to my parents and brother.
But they are gone, lost into the vast, endless eternity of smoke-
    filled, scarlet skies.

All we have is the mirror, to remember them by.
In the mirror, we see them smiling at us.
In the mirror we see our hopes.
In the mirror, we see our dreams, our memories.
Yet, in the mirror, we see ourselves running away from our past.

Who knew, that a shard of mirror will bind me to
My nightmares, yet comfort me with pleasant memories?

Who knew that I would call a mirror *'home'*... who knew?

AIMAN FAHEEM

Escape

This oil painting is titled 'escape' as it represents my personal space of finding escape in nature. The noise of this world often erupts an uncertainty in my heart and spreads to the choices I make in my life. However, reflecting upon the simplicity and perfection of nature allows me to revive the lively spirit I once had. At times of loss in hope, I instinctively found peace in trusting the free mind to take me to a place of optimism. These weren't merely tubes of paints that I used, rather the sole sources of sparing me breaths when life was suffocating me. Thus, this composition, and the act of painting in general, have a lot to do with preserving my sanity in a world filled with overwhelming sound.

JAYLON PASCUAL

My Way

Often I find myself thinking about wanting to change who I am
I wish I could be someone I'm not because I'm simply not
    satisfied with who I am now
I wish I could be kinder
I wish I could be more pretty
I wish I could be more expressive

I compare myself to others
It's not healthy I know but it's something I do unconsciously
    against my will
I'm not as kind as him
Not as pretty as her
Not as expressive as the ones I look up to

I sometimes catch myself thinking "why can't I just be normal"
Because these voices won't go away
I'm sinking deeper and deeper into a hole I can't escape from
I've been abandoned in space because no one can hear me and I
    can't breathe
"I just want to be normal" I yell but the noise can't travel out
    here

I choke
I can't breathe
I feel ice coating my skin making it hard to move
I can feel the warmth leaving my body and the cold seeps in
I close my eyes
When I realize

I was still on earth
I didn't go anywhere
I wasn't falling into a hole and I wasn't in space
It was all in my head
The way I viewed myself was all in my head
These insecurities were all in my head

The mind is a powerful thing
But its power can be good or bad

I decided to change my point of view
Started to think
I'm kind
I'm beautiful
I can be expressive if I want to be in my own way

It's hard to do at first and my negativity gets the best of me at
    times
But I keep pushing forward
I don't have to be normal
I can be weird and strange
I can be me
And if people don't accept me for it I don't care anymore

I'm tired of hiding
I'm tired of trying to change myself when I just can't
I don't want the real me to turn into a stranger
So I keep pushing forward
I decide who I am
I decide how I view myself
So I'm gonna live life my way

MATT LAU

The Calm After The Storm

Happiness to me is a temporary feeling when something good happens or when something funny happens. A mood. But to others, happiness is a state of well-being that encompasses living a good life—that is, with a sense of meaning and deep satisfaction. But when I'm taking photos, it all changes. I find happiness in taking photos of genuine moments. Capturing moments that feel pure and free. Whether it be with a person or an inanimate object there is a connection. A feeling between me and the subject there's always a story to be told behind a photo.

MATT LAU

Flower in the Daylight

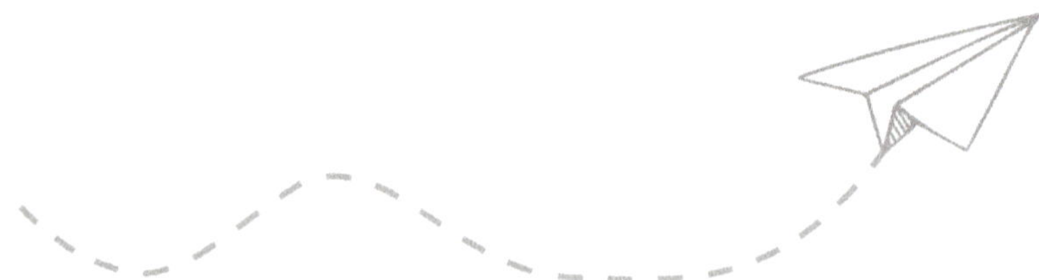

DHANBIR SINGH THETHI

Love is a Crime

How I became my own emotional culprit from a mere teenager

If love was a crime,
I would be on death row.

Each day and night,
I've begun to stay out of light
And hide this emotional plague
That I harbour deep inside.

I vowed to never succumb to it again,
As there was more loss to incur than gain
But I always break and watch my hopeless attempts
Continuously fail and go in vain

The first time I was arrested,
Who would have guessed?
That the bars of your heart,
Would leave me happily depressed.

When I met her, it was her smile.
A smile that I couldn't live without.
When her amber eyes met mine.
It was only elation that my heart could spout.

It was the first time ever,
That I had ever felt this way.
Didn't know if its conclusion would be exhilarating,
Or would it just leave me in the grays.

Finally had I gathered the guts and courage,
To carry out this emotional felony.
I approached the target and soulfully uttered the three magic
    words,

But who knew they would mark the beginning of the death of
	me.

I did it,
I loved.

Now for my actions,
There are consequences in front of me placed in lines.
I pleaded guilty but to no avail
I was tortured in ways which would send shivers down one's
	spine.

I thought I had been freed and I had learnt my lesson,
But who knew the desire of crimes only grows and does not
	lessen.

I committed the 'it' again.
Not twice, not thrice, but four times.
With more effort and dedication, I put in each time,
Only to return to the same prison for my continuous crimes.

From a bundle of freshly picked roses,
To finely written cards with poems from the bottom of my
	heart,
To the visions I had for her when I would hold her in my
	shackled arms,
Had all been foiled with the law-enforcing destiny, and we just
	grew apart.

Once you fall in love,
It becomes your addiction; you cannot live without it.
The more you attempt to separate yourself from this atrocity,
The deeper you get trapped in its bottomless pit.

If love was to be a crime,
I would be on death row.
However, this will be the one case where,
The prisoner does not want to be "let go."

DANA-KAYE MATTHEWS

Panic Attacks

Dear World,
Mental Illness is ubiquitous and relatable, it doesn't have to be taboo
It is important to discuss mental health and it doesn't have to be dramatic
or television-worthy to be real. I think that many people ignore their own
symptoms because they feel the need to cling to the notion that there is a
type of person who has mental health issues, and they are not that type. I
know people will find that they can relate to my description of my anxiety,
and that creates an avenue for healthy discussion.

The smell of rain makes my throat swell
My breath skitters weakly across my tongue
As my body shuts down
Preparing for the world to melt around me
My ears throb and my eyes turn inward
My fists are slamming helplessly against the roof of my coffin

I was 7 the first time my heart licked my heels
My blood squelching between my toes
Body cavernous and empty
We were learning about 'child prodigies'

A lesson, that, played backwards shrieked the Devil's anthem
You are **inadequate**
You are already behind
Mediocrity is an anvil that my young throat rejected
Its rancid aftertaste birthed unique tastebuds

My self-esteem has been bitten by angular nails
Who are always too close and hold too tightly
Who whisper with love, disguising arsenic in a velvet gift box

Tear trails trodden on too rarely
No one bothers to build a *damn*
The smell of rain is thick and suffocating

Eyes darting
Tornadoes behind my ears
Clenched hands
Autopilot is arduous
The itch is making its way up both sides of my neck
My left foot is filled with styrofoam
My forehead collapses into my nose

Frantic

My ribcage mimics the bagpipes of a hidden Scottish heritage
That I try not to think too hard about
I'm naked and quivering

It's well into the next day and I didn't sleep again
The arches of my feet are dull
Crescent moons tattoo the bags under my eyes

There's nothing wrong with me
There's *nothing* wrong with me
Prepare for the arrival of that pesky rain
No umbrellas
My hair deserves to be drenched
Gluing to my cheeks
I need to learn

GERALDINE SVIC

Sciamachy

'Sciamachy' represents the constant battle we all have between our most dark selves. The battle of fighting your inner demons and negativity. And the success of winning them over. It is the fragmentation and shattering of your darkest thoughts.

SURUTIGA RANJAN

Something More

In the midst of all that's wrong
Benevolence is lost
Mundaneness a kind neighbour
Nothing more than just a show

A creation of ignorance
Consequences denied
Flaws fabricated by perfection
In attempts at salvation

JUSTINA YANG

Fracture

"You know, it's funny; when you look at someone through rose-coloured glasses, all the red flags just look like flags."

Dear World... it's time to take off our rose-coloured glasses and see the news for what it really is—a cry for help

DOAA SHAIKH

Growing Pains

When I was three, I remember nobody wanting to sit next to me in the library. I thought that there was something wrong with me, but then I noticed the looks my mother got. Someone once told her to go back home, but I didn't know what that meant because London was home to me. Why did we have to go back to our apartment when Story Time hadn't even started?

When I was eight, I walked into a classroom in a little town in New Brunswick for the first time. "The class is getting bigger every year," was met with "and so are the girls." People asked me if I knew Saddam Hussein, or Osama Bin Laden, and if I could really speak English. I had a teacher ask me if I was from Africa, and another asked me what sorts of food "my people" eat. A year later, someone who I thought was my friend told me that my mother needed to stop wearing towels on her head. My parents didn't think being homeschooled was a good idea.

When I was 14, I lost my grandmother. I started seeing a man because I was vulnerable, and I didn't know any better. He called me exotic, like I was some sort of bird, but said because I was half-white I was acceptable. He called someone in my family a "dirty Paki" so often that I didn't realise it was a slur until he was long gone.

When I was 16, I knew that my parents would always be stopped at airports for not-so-random checks. This time, my parents were being checked for so long that we missed our flight out of London. There were raised voices, there were more slurs, and I realised for the first time that not everyone who asked to see my birth certificate had the right to. Our night at the hotel was paid for, and we left the next day. I haven't been home since.

When I was 18, I met another man whose words hurt less than anything I had heard before then. He talked to me about how he appreciated other cultures, how he was a believer in equality, how he couldn't believe that there were people who could abuse women. After a couple of weeks, he told me of how he ripped up Qurans at university to highlight inconsistencies, or how he told homeless people they were a waste of space. He left quickly once he realised I wasn't the exception, I didn't mourn because I didn't want to be.

When I was 22, I made peace with the fact that bad things happen to people. I finally understood that I didn't have to wait for people to leave me, I didn't have to keep giving people second chances. I realised that being used to racism was a coping mechanism to stop myself from being devastated every day. I stopped using my English middle name years ago, and I decided to stop introducing myself as Dee.

Shortly after I turned 24, I ended an old friendship with someone who told me that hijabs were disempowering. I bought my mother a hijab on New Year's Day.

KAY WU

Trim

SALLY CO

A Man's World

LUCY ZHANG

X, Y, Z

"The youth is the hope of our future" —Jose Rizal

KHYATHI RAO

I am (like) a girl

I am a girl.
    I
        Don't
            Have
                To
                    Be
                        Like
                            A
                                Girl
    I
        Don't
            Have
                To
                    Be
                  A
                        Puppet
                          Anymore
I don't have to eatlikeagirlsmilelikeagirlwalklikeagirltalklikeagirl
I don't have to be pretty, lean, fair, petite
I will not play the puppeteer—puppet game anymore
    Because
I have a ball of fire inside my heart
Growing fierier each day.
A ball of fire that tells me—
I don't have to be what you say
A ball of fire that tells me—
I have my own voice
That I am HUMAN!

I am a girl
                        Want
              I
          Whatever
      Be
     Can
   I
I am a girl

                          Dreams
                    Have
              Don't
          I
       Mean
     Not
    Does
  This
I will be like—
Amelia, who heard her heart
Emily Dickinson, who wrote her heart
Helen Keller, who wasn't blind to her heart
Saint Joan of Arc, who sacrificed with her heart
I will be me
    Because
I AM A GIRL WITH A BALL OF FIRE IN MY HEART

To all the girls—find your ball of fire.

CHARU SHARMA

Piazza San Marco

SELENA ZHOU

The Insignificance of a Grasshopper

After all, what more are we?

The waves will crash on glass shard stones
Like an angry flame burst on cedar wood
Like the pine smoke of young grass blades
They will crash and they will burn
But the waves will tune it out
She will walk on glass shard stones
Like a grasshopper amid green swords
She will walk through laughter and tears and mud
Like a baby, a newborn slate
And she will crash and she will burn
But the waves will wash her away
Like a shadow creeping up at dusk
To the glare of sun slapping down on buildings
Just the small things that we find so beautiful
They're very deadly indeed
But as they walk on grass shard stones
Like insects
They'll be washed away
Their imprint washed away
The waves will wash them
Away.

UROOJ SYED

Mosque

This is an acrylic painting of the Sultan Ahmed Mosque, otherwise known as the Blue Mosque.

MARIUM KHAN

Islamophobia: We Are Not Terrorists

Dear world, terrorists may identify themselves as Muslims, but terrorism goes against all teachings in the Islamic faith. Muslims are peaceful people. There will always be people who will be associated with you who are bad, but for every bad person there will be ten good ones, and they are the ones who truly matter.

I think that it's absolutely bomb,
not in a good way and no pun intended,
that our sad world has a "phobia"
for a religion of all things!
'ISLAMOPHOBIA.'
Defined as an irrational fear of Muslims and Islam,
a widespread fear that defines people like me as
Saddam or ticking time bombs.

WE ARE NOT TERRORISTS, WE ARE MUSLIMS!

Syria was once a beautiful country
now filled with innocent blood spilling
over the edges of the land and into the water
meanwhile the media still tries to convince you
that we're responsible for the slaughter?
A country of innocent Muslims being attacked for absolutely
no reason.

I just can't understand
the hate going back and forth
like a simple game of catch.
Whether its aggressive or passive
our world became depressive.
You say that we're progressive
but we're becoming regressive.

WAKE UP!
and realize that
I have no intention to mar, make scars, or blow up cars
I wouldn't shoot up an army base because
I might end up shooting my own father, brother, mother, sister

Oh and this cloth on my head?
I don't sleep with it on in bed,
or plan to blow up whatever it is you said.
This is called the hijab
it doesn't oppress
but gives freedom and protects.

Yet in airports when thousands of people walk right by
all you can see is me
a warning sign in the shape of a hijab.
You pat me down, checking to see
if I'm carrying any bombs,
looking for an excuse
to prove that terrorism is Islam.

I remember wanting to rip it off my head,
hand it to you and ask,
'Am I one of you yet?'

WE ARE NOT TERRORISTS, WE ARE MUSLIMS!

I am 10 years old,
about to go to Disney World
with my uncle.
Everything is fine
as I excitedly roll
my suitcase up to the X-ray machines
and get asked to show my passport.

I get pulled aside before I go
to retrieve my bag
because the worker seems to have seen me
as a big, red flag.
And it's all because my father's name is Muhammad,
the same name of one of the most respected
and religious men known in Islam—
Our Herald, Messenger, Prophet.
There's enough hatred in this world, so just stop it!
But NO,
to these people being related to a man
that sounds like he's related to Islam should be banned.

WE ARE NOT TERRORISTS, WE ARE MUSLIMS!

I beg of you to stop blaming me
for the mistakes of people who aren't even my kin.
Please try to see my point of view
and get to know me from within.

You think a simple ban will work, but trust me, it won't.
Because you can shoot, stab, bomb, break us—
We will not fall!

Hiroshima Nagasaki, Pentagon us—
We will not fall!
We will not fall like the Twin Towers you blame us for.

All I ask is that you stop all this hatred, judging, killing.
Trust me, all of this is possible,
but only if YOU are willing.

So I end this poem by saying
As-Salaam-Alaikum.
and even after everything,
may peace be upon you.

LUCY ZHANG

Shoshin

VAISHNAVY

Views From Below

AIKEN YONG

A Letter to My 15-year-old Self

I would like to dedicate this to a special person named Sunny. If I could go back 5 years and tell myself how things get better this is how I'd do it.

Dear Aiken,

Hey,
I'm Aiken, but like 20-year-old Aiken
Clearly 5 years from now your introductions are still awkward...
You still don't know if you should stick out your hand or not
And if you do shake their hand you still don't know when to
    stop
You still nervously laugh as your eyes shift and your cheeks get
    hot
You still don't know whether to say hi, or hey, but that don't
    matter a lot
Cause during introductions your tongue tends to be tied in a
    knot
But there's one thing that you have in your intros to strangers
    that I haven't got
And that's the fear of meeting new people

See, as you read this you probably figured I still write a lot,
But besides this its been over a year since I last wrote dude,
But don't worry: I still got it—the concepts not new
Your favourite thing to write about is yourself, and that's mine
    too
That's why I'm not writing about me, I'm writing about you
You're so selfless, and you write about yourself to make sure you
    still have some self left
You hope the words you write will teach you about yourself yes?
You performing is you telling yourself who you are cause its
    your best guess

So if you haven't figured it out yet
I don't write, cause I figured out who I am

I am a different man from the boy you see in the mirror
We may have the same face, but trust he don't look like me
We may be the same height, but he ain't all grown up like me
What changed that boy won't be pleasant for your ears
But his 'forever' turned into not even four years

Heartbreak will be a good test of whether,
You'll let your tears drop like rain, so you can say you're under
    the weather,
Or put the pieces of your heart straight back together
And realize that once you've hit rock bottom things can only get
    better

Dear Aiken, I know you joke a lot, but there'll be a time when
    life's not funny
You'll isolate yourself, but something amazing's waiting outside,
    just trust me
The best thing I ever did in these 5 years was break out of my
    shell, to see outside it was Sunny

Sincerely, You

ANANYA ANANTH

Ghost

This piece is a visual representation of what I feel listening to "Ghost," by Halsey.

ABEERA SHAHID

Another World

In another world,
I would be a bird.

Flying above water,
Through mountain peaks,
Believe in the sky's ability to carry.

Taking shelter in trees,
Finding home high,
Driving myself to new extremes.

Migrating to the down under,
No sense of direction,
Only intuition.

Eating Magpies,
So I can get by,
And renew my license to fly.

Stainglass windows,
Mirror my ride,
Teaching me from left to right.

To cockatoo I flock,
Hiding in tunnels
Built for criminals.

When darkness comes,
I befriend the bats,
Until it's time to curl up in my nest.

I hope to dream of another world tonight.

ANONYMOUS

After-Prom

"it tasted like chlorine and ketamine,"
i tell the girl from down the hall about my dreams
and the friends i'd kissed and pools i'd swim
she wore birkenstocks and a blue prom gown down to her knees.

last week it had all been daisy chains and rainbows
rose-tinted windows, backseats of stolen limos,
now it's pacing and making circles while she talks in her sleep
waking up to checking vitals and a detuned piano.

so pour more OJ in this robitussin (cough cough)
ask the doctors if they can up my dosage
i need a clean slate, some rollerblades, and an escape
be honest, doc. this place is scary when you're sober.

after-prom

SALEHA ANSARI

Serenity in a Seemingly Chaotic World

AMANDA JOY CEBALLOS LOPOS

"I remember being alone"

"I remember being alone" is a poem that I wrote based off of my personal experience with loneliness, and creative ways in which I learned to comfort myself, while denying my loneliness throughout the whole experience as I lacked the company of friends.

Back in grade 5, I designated a washroom stall to be my safe haven. My not so secret, secret hideout. My retreat for when I wanted to be alone. When I closed my eyes, I remember the sound. The walls echoing my voice back at me. It echoed through and through, touching each wall, almost sounding like a chorus of cries. A symphony of sadness even though I was the only one there, and no one was there to hear it but myself. The echo of my voice served as nothing but an illusion yet somehow it made me feel less alone.

I remember the look of the dirty mirrors. They looked like paintings of a girl whose cheeks were flushed rose. Her eyes were puffy and there were always tears rolling down her face, but no one was ever beside her. No one was ever crying for her or reaching out to hold her shaky hands. I realized that I was just staring at myself right when the salty tears stung my own dry lips. I liked that I could cry and the mirrors would always be watching. The mirrors never spoke to me, yet somehow, they made me feel less alone. I even had a little book. I wrote in it every single day. That book was my remedy. I wrote in that book just as often as you probably talked to your friends. But I didn't have those friends. I crafted that book to be my friend.

Replacing faces with pages was pathetic, yet somehow, it made me feel less alone. Because I was tired of being alone. I was trying to claw my way out of being alone. The word "alone" makes my stomach turn and wring itself. It dips under my skin and tears my insides apart. I tried to get help but my voice would just sink back into my throat, my tongue was weighted. No one knew what to do with me, not even myself. I remember all of it so clearly. The echoes, the dirty mirrors, the washroom stall, the book. They were so familiar. But now I don't need them like I desperately did before. Those days are gone. I'm not alone.

JAYLON PASCUAL

Synonyms for Depression

When did being edgy become a synonym for depression
Since when was being depressed cool
Since when did having mental illnesses and disorders become a
　　new trend

People act as if depression and other mental illnesses is a joke
Maybe they do it to make a heavy topic seem a little lighter
　　maybe they do it to make it easier to talk about
Either way it sometimes comes off as rude and insensitive
Because these topics are not a joke

People suffer from these illnesses everyday they can't function
　　properly because of it and it hinders their life all the time
People take it lightly
Use it as an excuse
But these things shouldn't be used as excuses
The way people treat them nowadays makes it seem as though
　　these illnesses don't really exist but they do
And they are a huge problem in the human population

But no they're brushed aside
Used as cool new trends
It comes to the point where people think others are being
　　"edgy" to be cool when they're not
They're actually hurting inside
Trying to communicate what they're going through but people
　　just think they're being "edgy"
This is what causes people to bottle up their emotions
This is what causes them to keep quiet
Because society these days is so ignorant and oblivious that
　　people can't tell a joke from a literal cry for help

Humans are social creatures we live in communities and yet
    we're so oblivious to the feelings of those who surround us
If someone looks troubled ask why they're troubled
If they say "It's nothing I'm fine" but they still look upset push a
    little harder
Because that small push might get them to open up to you
Don't just write then off as edgy because you're just adding to
    their suffering
You're kicking them while they're already down
You might not want to address the problem but I will

This poem is for the people suffering in silence
For the ones who are too nervous or scared to speak their mind
Who think they're alone even though they're surrounded by
    people
For the ones who find it hard to get up in the morning because
    they think there's no hope
For the ones who lie awake at night because they're just
    thinking way too much
For the ones who look at the world through clouded eyes and
    they just need someone to give them a tissue
This poem is for the people who are called edgy when they're
    actually suffering
For the ones who are misjudged because of a problem they
    didn't choose to have

As for the others
Just help them get back up
Because if you were in the place you would want another person
    to do the same for you

CHARU SHARMA

Untitled

SHOFFANA SUNDARAMOORTHY

Unfinished

In his perfect world,
Perhaps his mind would have been at ease
Just knowing exactly why.

Truth be told,
He never truly comprehended
Why a wave of tranquility surged
At the thought of seeing her.
In reality, she would have
Left that following night.

It's a shame you just suddenly left
And stopped remembering him,
Cause he lost a precious soul,
His guardian angel.

It's complicated.
It was just...

In a perfect world,
He would have forgotten her
The way she couldn't recall him.

But perfection doesn't exist.
He misses you.

Then again,
It doesn't matter how he felt.
It never did.

He doesn't regret anything.

In all honesty,
You brought to his
Attention that he needs to stop
Hanging onto things he
Thought could surpass time,
No matter how much he worries
About your well being
Which is ironic cause
His first home was in
That womb of yours

Nevertheless,
He learnt to let that collapse
And just sprout his own roots,
To form his own base,
From the destroyed ruins.

Thanks to you,
He finally grew up.

Things can change,
Maybe not how he intended
But how they should be.
Besides, he can see
Through his own eyes.
What he sees in front of him
Is a loving, supportive group
Of friends and neighbours.

Someday, you may finally
Be ready to come and stay
With him till death does you in.
That would be unfortunate
Considering he's no longer
Your little boy, mother.

You

you is about the love i have for my girlfriend and
how being with her saved my life

you were a hit of sun, in the midst of the biggest storm to ever
    exist,
you were the one thing that gave me an ounce of hope
you hit me so hard, i didn't even realize i was struck,
by your soul.
for once in my life i realized that maybe there was more to life
    than just umbrellas and raincoats,
that maybe for once in my life i could take off my clothes, and
    feel warm again,
that it was okay to show a little skin,
and that i shouldn't fear the sun's rays,
and sunburn was not the worst thing to ever exist.
that it was okay to feel something.
You showed me that pain was just my brain telling me that that
    something didn't feel right.
you showed me that pain was temporary and love lasted a
    lifetime,
you showed me how storms don't last forever
and the sun will always come out tomorrow,
you showed me that love stories had some truth to them
and that it was okay to write my own.
you hit me so damn hard i swear to god a part of me that was
    broken, fixed itself,
the part I've been forever longing to find, was brought back by
    an angel in white
and i swear to God i thought i almost died.
i thought i almost died.
i thought it was too good to be real.
you showed me that it was okay to live,
and how it was not okay to want to die.

how it wasn't okay to pick up the blade even though you can feel
    it trace your skin in your mind
even though you can feel the overwhelming feeling of pain leave
    your body
how you could feel the cold metal touch your wrist
you showed me there were much better things to do.
you showed me that it was okay to kiss my scars because they
    put me back together
after i broke myself apart.
you showed me that it was okay to eat food because no matter
    how much i weighed
the love you had for me weighed much more
that no amount of food could ever make me hate myself
that it was okay to be hungry
because it didn't make me fat.
you showed me that it was okay to look forward to tomorrow,
    and how it was okay to be happy.
you showed me that in order to find peace you must go through
    war,
you showed me that it was okay to pick my battles,
and my god i would fight for you forever.
You were the sun shining through the darkest cloud,
and i took off my jacket and i felt your warmth on my skin,
i felt you kiss my face and left imprints of your love
as my skin goes from white to pink
i knew it was okay to feel again.

SANAZ BANI

Outgrown

KAY WU

Silence

AIMAN FAHEEM

An Unjust Nation

This poem tells the story of the unjust mind many amongst us carry in suppressing the voices that arise in support of those who happen to be of the female gender. This poem isn't targeting anyone or any ideology specifically but is composed to awaken the paralyzed mind in seeing beyond what is simply seen.

A priceless soul, an unjust nation
Her last smile was spiritless and sideways
The panic and fear she held in her eyes
The blue bruises she had on her thighs
All that remained was a blood-stained event
That trashed the duration my sister spent
Our dancing dreams for vacation
Took an atrocious 360-degree rotation
That day, my sister headed out for the mall
She wore the usual high heels to look tall
And one of those see-through tank tops
From mainly expensive-brand shops
Wanting an adventure, she went by foot
Carelessly skipping along while their eyes stayed put
They scanned her from head to toe
The mall only a block away, when they said hello
The five men, with awfully menacing gaze
She described them as, "Dogs who hadn't had food for days"
Shortly realizing she was being followed
The last bit of saliva she swallowed
Scorching sweat, and her loud heartbeats
They chased her through narrow streets
Becoming a victim of the group of men
She prayed for strength and said her last amen
Experiencing what every girl dreads from
She returned home looking very glum

With only a cloth over her cold figure
Circumstances I struggled to configure
Her shivering hands wrote the heartbreaking event
She handed the torn paper, and ran out for her final torment
It read, "I'll be dead by tomorrow"
My baby sister! She left me only to sorrow
I then reread her last line "Justice will prevail
When safety will not need a veil"
A priceless soul, an unjust nation

ANGELA HE

Help Me...

SEERAT REHMAN

Standstill

i speak in tongues yet know no words.
i think in colours, in sounds, in peaks and valleys.
you can try, but you will not reach me.
you can't see it but my chest houses Pandora's Box.
my heart is chaos,
my lungs are anarchy,
and this world is too much for me,
and this world is too much for me.
their cyanide smiles hint at disappointment,
their thoughts of "here we go again."
i was here - i swallowed fire and let out the smoke
and died by my own hand.
shards of reality fall like snow
dusting the evergreens with the definition of
immortality in our small infinities.
in this way, i'm still here, and you will always be here
and silent glades stretch beyond us
but the birds took flight before the storm.

GERALDINE SVIC

Terra Mater

"Terra Mater": Represents the beauty in the tarnishing of mother nature. The same way sometimes we feel tarnished ourselves, and often forget to realize the silver lining within the tarnishing. She represents the beauty in the broken. and a reminder to look at the brighter side of things.

JORDAN CURRIE

Wishing Well

a woman is a well
all cobblestone walls and silent ripples
an abyss to toss unwanted pennies into
but a safe place to sip from

something to wish upon
something to pursue

descending buckets and cupped hands
collecting nourishment
take
take
drink
drink
and when their roughened knuckles hit the empty bottom
and scrape the surface dry,
they'll wait for the refill.
they know they'll always get more

what a versatile appliance
one who gathers your scrapheap
off the bottom
but possesses the time to provide
to filter out the grime
good enough for you to drink

press your ear
listen down closely
and the ripples begin to resemble a heartbeat

this well is alive
will always create more even when you hoist
the water away from her
this well thirsts
collects when rain falls and spills it
out of cracked stone lips (and we keep drinking)
this well wishes on herself
gathers the discarded coppers
and moulds them into gold

a woman is a well. a woman is
not a well.

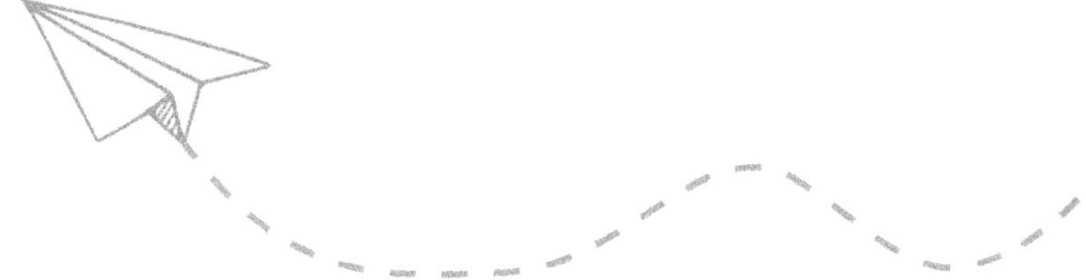

AARON CHUA

Jester

Curtains drawn
The soundtrack is a symphony of the percussion of my heartbeat
    and the rhythm of my breathing
The eyes gaze towards my direction but hopefully not at me
To be the centre of attention is a dream for many people
I prefer the edges of the room where my closest friends are the
    walls that meet at the corner
Front and centre on the stage is foreign to me
The blinding spotlight blankets me in a light of humiliation
The audience stares, their glares pierce through my paper-thin
    persona
The pause lingers through the air
The anticipation of "what will he do?"
My mouth opens but no words come out
She will laugh
Because the frog in my throat leaves me at a croak
And my words unformed because the cat has made my tongue
    its plaything

Day-to-day conversation is an endeavour
It is a performance that is judged by the spectators
The royalty whose opinions matter
A mere wish to ask of a genie
Is to have the ability to converse with the Princess
A mockery I make of myself just by fantasising
The devil on my shoulder that says "just walk up to her"
Instantly addressed by the angel with "don't or else you will be
    embarrassed"

She would not talk to a person like me
Because that's not how the world works
There is a hierarchy and equilibrium to be maintained
She is a princess she wouldn't share pleasantries with a peasant.

She mingles with men that matter and not mongrels such as I
I should not intoxicate myself with "what ifs" and scenarios
I can't even be bothered on the "yets"
Despite my insistence on "I haven't talked to her yet"
It is a poorly kept secret that "yet" is never happening
Because I am in bondage of chains that are made of my doubts
    and insecurities
Left to rot in a dungeon of "what ifs" and never coming "yets"

I fantasise that I could make her swoon
To find out that she isn't with anybody else
And it will be happily ever after
Like a Disney fairytale
My reality is the Brothers Grimm
It will end in misery, disappointment, and heartache
Because even in a fairytale about my life
I am nothing but a side character left to the mercy of the
    background.
I imagine that I could win her over with a performance because
I imagine that I have a knack for words
I imagine that I would give a "Performance so good that She had
    hoped she would have recorded it to listen to it again"
I imagine that I was proper

The Princess
Already feels like a synonym of don't bother trying
A little fantasising doesn't hurt
And fantasies they shall stay because She is royalty
and I am but a jester made to make a fool of himself

ANISHA MEHRA

Upside Down

SURUTIGA RANJAN

Someday

Someday
The sun will rise
To light the sky blue

Someday
The winds will calm
The storms that brew inside

Someday
The children will learn
Not everything is pure

Someday
The people will believe
No line exists to divide

Someday
The wars will end
Mind and body both

Someday
The stars will shine
In possibility of hope

Someday
The moon will rise
In reflection of the light down below

EMILY MCDOWELL

I Hate You

I hate you is about the time i was raped by my best friend.

let me remind you
it wasn't your face
that sent me into a spell
it was the words you spoke
that would bring me from
white to pink
thinking that maybe you
saw more than just my anatomy.
It was your hands
that sent me into a dark place
that brought me from
pink to white
in fear.
as your hands glazed over my
delicate body, and found its way
to my breasts
it wasn't your face that made me cry
it wasn't your words that made me scream
it was you.
it's you in my head at 3 in the morning
telling me that if i let you borrow me
for an hour, then maybe
you would love me more.

it was you in your black car,
driving me wherever i wanted,
only if i placed my soft hands over your body
until you told me to stop.

Let me remind you that it will be me
who sees more than your face and your words.
Let me remind you that i see you.
the one who took no as a challenge,
and who had mistaken my screams
for pleasure.

VALENTINA CABALLERO

"Just Be Yourself"

CAROL MARKOS

For Before

For my ancestors. For my children. For my people.

I am horrible at taking care of plants
In the twelfth grade I bought my first two
An African Violet I named Genevieve
And a tropical leaf named Cecile
I picked them because there were words like resilient
And hardy
on the labels
That didn't end up working out
And I only buy cacti now
Those ones are supposed to be
indestructible
Supposed to be
I wonder what it must feel like for my house plants
To be labelled with words like
resilient
and hardy
And indestructible
And still be dying while nobody notices
I wonder if that's the perfect metaphor for what being Coptic[***]
    is like
It is Palm Sunday
April 9th, 2016
Here I am
Waking up
One body
Oversized t-shirt
Baggy pajama pants
4 different species of cacti dying outside my bedroom door
Here were are
Forty three bodies
Cardigans on tetas[**]

Dresses on daughters
43 different ways to take a last breath
And all I've got to show for it
is this feeling in my bones
I'm sorry
I don't know how to make poetry from shockwave
I can't imagine what it must have looked like in the first
    moments when the incense met the smoke
I wonder if anyone kept praising after the bomb went off
I wonder what that would have sounded like
I don't know how to tell you that I know 43 people I have never
    met
That I can imagine myself there
Picking up my brother's Tonia*
Following the gold embroidery to each bloodstain
Like string on a crime investigation board
I wonder
If I follow far enough
Will I see a picture of who's responsible
Will I get an array of likely suspects
Will I find crime scene pictures, picked apart to the last breath
    someone took while their chest was still their chest
Before their chest stopped being their chest
Before it became
Evidence
Something happened here
Someone's something happened here
Someone's last something happened here
And my chest is still my chest
My lungs still have enough air to speak with
How dare my lungs still have enough air to speak with
How dare I not write a poem for every piece of evidence
On every roll of caution tape
You are telling me it is not safe here
You are telling me it is not safe in my own home
You are telling me to stay out

I am telling you—
I am inviting you in
I am holding my hands open to a world
That only knows fist
I want to tell you this story while my tongue is still my tongue
While my chest is still my chest
Before
I am evidence

---

*A Tonia is a traditional dress that males wear in ceremonies
**teta means grandma in Egyptian Arabic
***Coptic people are the Indigenous people of Egypt

JACKI SHI

Metamorphosis

DOAA SHAIKH

On Curry and Forgetting Problems in the Face of Better Things

Trying to remind myself of how politics works
While leg cramps remind me of the night before
And I'm trying my hardest to stay awake
On this morning's 44.

My student came to me with complaints, again
A guy she turned down told her smelled like curry—
Legislative, Executive, Judicial, I hope she remembers that—
I always tell her that university has a lot more to offer than just
    men.

The first time I heard the curry joke, I didn't get it
And if I'm honest, I still don't.
Curry is delicious, deep, divine—
The bus honks at a passing driver.

She has a midterm in a few days;
Canadian politics is so bizarre.
I think everyone forgot about the problems
Because red was better than blue this time, and no one aims for
    the stars.

I change my mind, problems are further from people's minds
    than stars are.
At least everyone looks at the stars.
When was the last time I read about Reconciliation?
What are we doing about Syria?
Why does Toronto have so many homeless and what are we
    doing about it?
Why are we excusing disastrous relationships and ignoring
    human rights violations?
Why—

I meet my student
Her uncertainty hides behind new glasses.
We review politics, I'm reminded why I studied biology.
She asks me if she can take me to her classes.

She's tired of listening to people glorify our government
"We just keep talking about his hair."
Dear world, dear Canada, remember our problems,
And stop talking about his hair.

HAILEY TSOLAKIS

Reclaiming Girlhood

"Me (Age 4) & Me (Age 20)" is a companion piece to the poem
"Reclaiming Girlhood."

The first time a man
Commented on my body
I was five years old.

I can't remember
What was said, but it felt like
Destiny for me

To be standing there
Unquestionably and still,
Until dismissal.

Like my entire
Blood line had this memory
Of violation

Burned into their bones,
And his voice weighed on my back
Like centuries did.

I've always had this
Acute awareness of it:
The misogyny.

And how unspecial
My girlhood full of shame was.
I'm tired of it—

Talking about all
The times men have made me
Wish I could drop dead

And take them with me.
Why is womanhood defined
By counting assaults?

I've had my years of
Convergence with other girls,
Trading tragedies;

Lamenting over
Why I could not stop it from
Happening to me.

Too much of my life
Has been sacrificed at the
Hands of this crisis.

A few years ago
I started a mission of
Autonomy, so

I stand a pillar
Every day, unwilling to
Condone my murder.

When I think of my
Body, I think of the love
That I cultivate;

Of all the goodness
I bring into the world, not
Of the men that take.

This has become my
Vindication: believing
That I own myself;

Feeling the fullness
Of every breath and loving
My recovery.

HAILEY TSOLAKIS

Me (Age 4) & Me (Age 20)

KELLY ESTOMO

Do It Yourself (DIY)

*Tales of the ever-changing role of a kid and where they belong in the world,
what kinds of love are out there, and more specifically, the frustration of a
woman of colour in the music scene.*

When I tell you that music occupies the negative space in my
    body,
that the nylon strings are a punching bag,
that every song is a documented therapy session,
that I've carved into the surface of its future and saw a glimpse
    of myself there,

I don't want to hear
"You don't study music. You don't have what it takes."

Have you ever studied a tiny 5th grader attempt to stretch her
    frame over the body of a grown acoustic? Or watched her
    toothpick fingers make imaginary shapes down its neck?
    Would you be afraid that she'd break like twigs from how
    strongly she was shaking?

She went on to study boys fronting rock bands, and sung her
    research papers like Sarah McLachlan.

She studied the length of her hair, and how hard it was to chop
    the back side of her head without a second mirror.

She studied popular lead singers, so she tried performing like a
    boy, tried screaming but couldn't, and after years of writing
    melodies too softly, she never learned how to yell.

She took up DIY hair dying. Hid boys' boxers under skinny girl
    jeans.

And maybe this helped me strum my acoustic a little harder.

But all I've been asked is if I was

a) okay, or
b) gay.

Somehow those two melted into each other till I couldn't tell
    which was which.

I've been running away from The Small Asian Girl because Small
    Asian Girls don't scream over electric guitars.

Do you know what dudes with a headstock for a brain call that?

"Too loud, step away from the mic."
"That's hot, but maybe tone it down."
"Are you trying to be a female (Asian) Kurt Cobain?"
"Study something else."

My studies show that:

1) It's not enough to look like a dude, or play like a dude,
2) It's not enough when I'm told that the songs I write use the
    same 4 chords,
3) It's not enough when I'm still too afraid to tell a man how
    much I love music,
because I DON'T LOVE IT ENOUGH.

My friend fronts her own band. Someone asked her backstage if
    she was a groupie.

Some days, I say,
"At least I have that."
And some days, I say,
"I will drill the silhouette of a Filipino Canadian girl into the
    basement of my abandoned local venue with the butt
    of a cheap microphone, and shout my bloodcurdling

inadequacies into its abyss. And when the echo drains itself, I'll pick up any guitar and strum anything (for nobody in particular), coo like a bird too early in the spring morning, and swim in my own reverb, while the boys with headstock brains drown in the very art they make."

[Tracy Bonham] once said, "Guitar-wise, I have a certain style that I can't seem to get any guitar player to mimic, and it's because they're good and I'm bad," she has said. "And I don't mind. There's a way I want to hear it, so I just do it myself." (Wikipedia)

KELLY ESTOMO

The Most Human Love

*I'm in love with the idea that people make movies to make you feel
something. I wish I was human enough to do that on my own.*

Don't tell me how to fall in love!
Now I don't know what it really is!!
Or the thousands of ways it can manifest!!!

Like
when you ask me if I'm leaving when I'm just going to the
    restroom,

Like
when you're getting mad at me for hating myself,

Like
when I check for the rise and fall of your chest at night,

Like
when you tell me I was in your dream that one time.

Oh,
I guess love is imminent.
So now I'm just a speck on a
spinning mobile ceiling fan,
trying to grasp what certain feelings are supposed to feel like.

Oh,
I guess it's hard to reduce human nature down to something
    digestible.

I love that love is several people,
seen through several lenses,
a different skin to the loving touch;

I'll hold you for that universal warmth.

WARWICK PANG

Arashiyama Bamboo Forest, Kyoto Japan

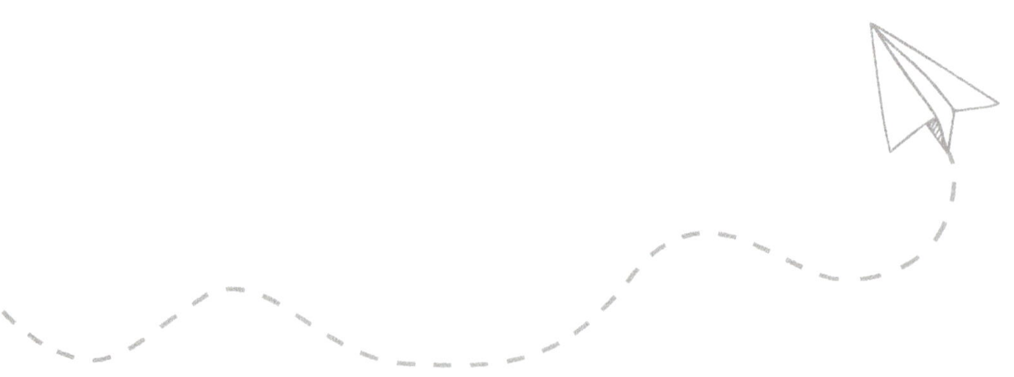

AYANA SIDDIQUI

I Wish You Weren't

i wish you weren't the sun—
because we both know i burn too fast,
and shielding my sunburnt eyes only messes with your golden
　　heart.
where i cast shadows, you flood with light,
and when i'm dragged from the shallows, you keep me in sight.

i wish you weren't the moon—
because i can't bring myself to wait for you all alone in the dark,
with tomorrow holding no promise of together, and tonight
　　keeping me under the weather.
but when i'm drowning in waves of blue velvet and you're the
　　only rock for miles,
you make me want to stay.

i wish you weren't the skies—
because it's getting harder and harder to look up, much less
　　crane my neck for hours on end.
i cannot find all of you all at once,
and when my feelings come in fragments, it's hard to count by
　　the thousand.

i wish you weren't the universe—
because there's nothing that makes me feel smaller than your
　　definitive existence.
where you stand your ground, i stumble and run from port,
and while you have worlds to offer, i always turn up short.

but if this is really you, then i wish i could be like this, too.

AREEB ATHAR

13,000 Feet in the Sky

Look Up

Look up.
Has anyone ever said that to you?

In a world of DMs, texting and more,
In the realm of your 'lol's or 'rolling on the floor'
Head down, gadgets out,
That's what life is all about.

We all know the phrase, 'get off your phone!'
'Put it away, leave it alone!'
But let's be honest, who'd rather listen to someone drone
On and on about nothing of note?

So take out your phone, look through the screen
Use your camera to capture what your eyes could have seen.
Watch a video instead of making a memory
Because that's what it is to be happy and free.

Focus your gaze on the pixels that show
All that you'll ever *really* need to know
Who cares to enjoy freshly fallen snow
When you can catch up on reruns of your favourite show?

What's more important than the world that you hold
In the palm of your hand, metallic and cold?
You don't need to *talk* to the person next door,
Just send them a text, it's quick and secure.
Who could ever ask for more?

Embrace impersonality, don't waste your time
Engaging with people when you can socially climb
On the eternal walls of Facebook and Twitter
Anyone who thinks otherwise is just being bitter

But while in the midst of your digital haven
Without which your life would undoubtedly cave in
You might miss the small things that make life so remarkable
Unless you look up.

ANGELA HE

Stuck in a Screen

MELANIE KLINGEL

The Core of a Woman

SALEHA ANSARI

Played Like Puppets

Played like puppets.
Entangled in our demise.
Fighting to escaPE -
our so called para-digms

Societal pressure, and daily judgement,
Taking a toll on our sequestered minds.
FAILING and FLAILING while tryna find a way out,
Obligated to conform. Assimilate, Adapt, n Normalize.
Flowering our lives like ornate decor.
Blinded. Needless to say, we still require so much more,
Played like puppets.

Actions controlled,
Thoughts twisted taking terrifying turns.
Authoritative powers grabbing towards our final hopes,
Seizing the last inch of our self-control.

Played like puppets.
Us helpless humans. Grabbing hold of oneself while finding a
    way out.

Clinging onto a ledge, tryna suppress our loud shOUTS

Constantly controlled yet carelessly trudging on.
Frame inside frame, box inside box.
Played like puppets.

Unaware but still surviving…what more could we really ask for?
Revitalizing power and just holdin' on for longer.
No change. No frantic cries to be heard in the pitch-black nights
    of our world.

Held back by our limits, our boundaries, the strict
    misrepresentation.
Casting shadows on our judgment, this terrible
    misconstruction.
hovering like clouds and blocking the light of day
Unaware

Unaware, and Played.
Stoppin' n slammin' a brake, that's something we have yet to
    master
Shifting gears and reachin' out is also an important matter,
Played like Puppets.

Pollination raises fascination,
Murder deeming disgust and captivation,

Unsettled n disoriented, bewildered n fazed
This filter on our brains, our actions, and our lives.
Falsified.
Unaware.
Puppeteered…

STEVEN CHEUNG

Tiffany Blue

Emphasizing our perception of natural light versus artificial light

STEVEN CHEUNG

Double Vision

SEERAT REHMAN

Linger

the ides of october carry your name on the wind
and the old, chewed up pen caps bookmark your half-empty
    journals
in my mind, your ghost casts golden shadows across the ground
    you left cold

i see you in the scent of the green tea you loved
i see you in the dead leaves falling to earth
i see you in fading light
i see you in myself

and my clothes only fill half the closet
you left behind my favourite sweater
with a rose in the hood
but the thorns draw blood
without even touching the hand
that your fingers once waltzed across

for the lovers—to each, the other is exaltation
but the sun burned out and the world went black
and when I awoke, time had stopped and you had left

DEEKSHA CHAUDHERY

Tales of my eyes

If you look into my eyes
They will tell you stories
Tales of an unfinished romance, a broken heart,
a forgotten chance.

If you look into them again
you will see fear.
Fear of letting you know what you have already seen
those dark mysteries, those hidden tears
have already been revealed.

If you look again,
You may find hope.
Traces of a childlike look,
a heart plethoric of dreams.
A world full of joy, of friendship, love, candies and toys.

But if you look for the last time—
You will find them vacant.
Drained of dreams,
Of hope and love.
Because they have been betrayed too many times,
that they do not know where to look
and what to find

HEBA ALFAYEZ

Blunt Nature

SALLY CO

Lost in Translation

SADIA SHEIKH

Gezelligheid

Borders don't have to divide us.

Smears on trains in the silent night
the soil arranged to wed the blood
papers signed in unsteady hands
with freedom's heads they filled them
they armed the
children to fight
their
fathers.
Eyes swayed, they craved, they caved:
I have blood across the border.
I make love across the border.
I draw blood across the border.
I fly doves across the border.
I give blood across the border.
I am home across the border.
I owe blood across the border.
There's a throne across the border.
A king to be overthrown.
Hatred sprouts in fairy circles
so there must be hope.
And they promptly
armed our children
to fight
their
fathers.
Itchy land; hungry for death,
decomposition,
rebirth,
more wars.

DEEKSHA CHAUDHERY

The Desert Dreamer

Where do all the lost things go
where does that beautiful river flow?
I can't see anything here,
this barren land of sadness and despair
where the world is empty,
where the land is crisscrossed with many cares
and the children have so much to bear.

But, even in this land, you will find hope
the barefoot young lad running through the dry slope
who is happy even in turmoil!
whose hopes and dreams continue to thrive,
Not bothered by the dried streams or sandy soil
he lives in a world of his own, which no one can uncoil.

His dreams are birds that love to fly!
As small little children, we have lived this carefree world
how different were our lives, free of cares, devoid of strife!
playing into the moonlit nights, singing and dancing to our
    heart's delight!

Then what happened to us that we stopped doing everything we
    loved?
We should all live our childhood again!
Let's give our dreams another life, let them reach greater
    heights,
Let's erase everything and make it white, to make another
    verve, cheerful and light!

FIONA YANG

Carnage

SADIA SHEIKH

Mouth: Open, Close

How do I prove I lived? How can I give myself a voice? Do they want to hear my voice? Would I want my kids to hear my voice?

Mouth: Open, Close
When I pass my people in the street, I gaze past them like I can't see them. I find the women in their traditional clothing particularly offensive, even as I find myself a symbol of protest when I wear it. I recognize in their eyes the same continuous tolerance as in my parents'. As my mother so often reprimanded me, there's no use fighting about everything. But I knew that somewhere deep inside, a rage bubbled, at the moment dampened by love, but which one day would inevitably come free. One day, I would open my mouth and not shut it until I'd hurled back equivalent insults to the ones my parents—my people—I'd—received throughout my life.

—

Increasingly aware of the fact that whatever we said to her would shape the lens through which she viewed the world, alongside being self-proclaimed 'woke,' I found it very difficult to answer her questions without falling into hypocrisy. The truth was, I hadn't solved most of the fundamental dilemmas she presented, but the worst part was that I could no longer blindly hate her, knowing what I did about her parents and having met the older versions of her in my own life. I hated being in the grey, and as I got older, I found less of life to be black and white, which, to put it simply, upset the ease with which I wanted to live it and formulate my opinions.

—

My knees hurt as I ran, as I exercised, and when I worked out with him, I was unnecessarily fragile. I think I'd begun to think of myself as delicate, as the delicate girl of my dreams from when I was thirty pounds heavier. A thin-minded girl trapped in a fat-bodied girl; it was a nightmare. Nowadays, I force myself to look in mirrors, to work out in front of them, to watch how my body works to ensure I survive. To think I used to starve it not only of food, but thanks.

KAY WU

Overthinking

VERONICA MONTECALVO

Enough

It took me a long time to get to where I am today,
Where the world isn't just black and white but grey
Always surrounded by negativity
Where calling yourself ugly is normal
Where believing you are beautiful is vain
Seeing skinny girls on magazines, drunk girls on TV
And sad girls
Everywhere

Expectations we can't live up too
Expectations that are sky high
And we are on our toes trying to touch the clouds
But we can't reach them
We will never be able to

I was fourteen when I started to believe I was beautiful
It was only because he told me I was

I never thought I was enough
Pretty enough
Smart enough
Athletic enough

Living in a generation
Where seeking the approval from others is more acceptable
Than looking in the mirror and accepting yourself

Positivity is looked down upon
When we should be cheering each other on
But here we are in 2018
Fighting the same problems as every generation before us
And we're stuck
Stuck because young girls are raised to think

They can't be doctors. They have to be a princess
Where a man will sweep her off her feet and make her feel
    beautiful
When sweetie, you can feel beautiful without him

I am seventeen now
And I am enough

I don't need him to tell me I'm beautiful
Because I know I am
I am independent and driven
And I will personally deserve everything I am given
I don't need a man who just wants to play
I'd rather have my career that will never walk away someday

Everyone is beautiful
Its hard for people to realize their self worth
Because there's such high standards on earth
But I promise you
You are enough

AMIRA BOUCHEMA

Between Us

Between us
There was never a difference
But a distance turned into miles
To overcome

If I said I did not have an attachment to phone booths
I would be lying through my teeth and nothing more
And perhaps this should not be so
Yet I still do

The very thought of you
Was an exhilarating breath of life,
A breath to awaken all lives
The murderers and martyrs alike

And even with phone calls
Your breath somehow travels faster than the wind
Through waves of sound invisible to the eye
Magic made from fairies rather than light and science

Me holding the receiver as though I was holding your hand
In the miles that we were apart in
The love crossing seas and skies
Oh if you knew how much it meant to me

I had wasted the small 25 cent coins
Desperate to hear your voice
Phone cards in the desperation
To hear your lips utter sounds

In the bright red cage that I claimed as mine
I talked hours on end
Same time same place

Desperate for the routine

While I ran wild and free
I loved the feeling of warmth that the red cage gave me
To believe in fate

Because Fuck free will
Watch me dump it in The Beaches
With the rain kissing my skin
And the sunlight gone

I miss phone booths
Hiding in those small cabins when it's raining
The dim lighting over the register
The beeping on the line

The shadow of my hands hovering on the receiver
The pressure on the keypad
The twirling of the cord as I listened to you thoughtfully
The jingling of coins in the deep pockets of my coat

The shuffling of old leather boots and high knee socks.
My cold numb fingers
Sweet scratchy voices
Cigarette in hand and endless tales to tell

Sadly
Recently
Truly
And seriously

I have been hearing the same voice
The same sentence
Of your voicemail
I did not have the courage to cancel your line

I'm sorry

But I held on to you too dearly
Those phone calls
Now when I put the coins in
It's nothing but the same voice
The same words

No variation
No laughing

I miss phone calls
Now when I make phone calls
They have no meaning
And only need
Nothing more and nothing less
Just requirements
Only eating my time for unhappy means

Now the red cage has been broken
And you let me go free
A bird that doesn't know how to fly or flee

A bird whose wings you've broken
With the difference
The distance between you and me

MIHO NAGAYAMA

Take a Break

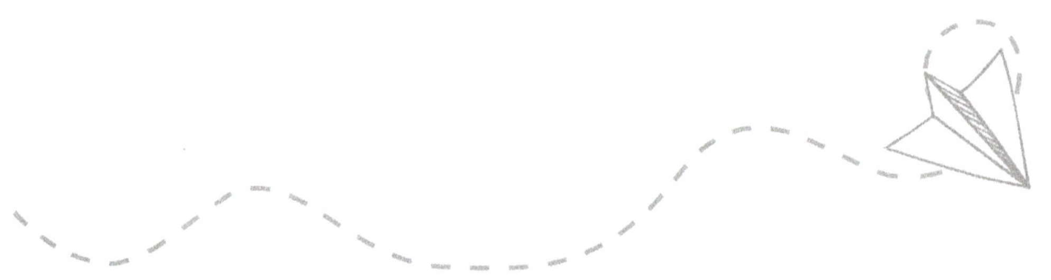

DANIELLA SERRADOR

Prickly Pear

Someone needs to make a word
For that queer thing the people do
When they insist, insist, insist
That something, their thing, must be true.
Their assertion, they assert, is vital.
Lend an ear or two.
For a battlecry, a call to action
You heard their passion, then you knew.

Someone must invent a word
To capture the frenzy of the crier.
Their sparking, fierce, voluptuous words
Shall form their opposition's pyre.
And as you listen to their speech
Your heart lifts higher, higher, higher.
Regardless of your thought at first
You're taken in; now grows the fire.

Round up the poets, get them quick!
Buckle in, make them invent
A word for this phenomena.
Let letters represent.

See, the shouter does no more than shout.
These 'leaders' never act.
"Attack!" they cry, "Attack! Attack!"
Their hands shall not react.

Someone, please, just find a word!
This world needs one, I cry.

Oh me? Why don't I make one up?
Heh.
Not a job for I.

KANEERA UTHAYAKUMARAN

Thoughts

These are two short poems representing two struggles humans face; our environment and regret. We often neglect the fact that no matter what, the earth is the only place that we can call our home, and forget to live our lives to the fullest.

The truth is that we have broken the earth beyond repair.
See, the heart can be broken and emptied yet still, it is there.
But the earth has been shattered,
and it is the definition of unfair.
How could we take such a large, beautiful gift for granted?
A world with water and clean air.
We polluted all that was once clean.
We took away all that was given to us.
We destroyed it all.
And now we fuss,
when there is no hope for this world anymore.
No matter how many speeches on global warming we can say,
the destruction of the earth is underway.
A thousand trees can be replanted,
but we all know,
that we took this world for granted.

Regret

At thirteen laps around the sun,
I'm already thinking about what I haven't done.
When I die,
I will not think about all the things I have done,
But all that I didn't.
 Too often, in our final moments before death,
We feel nothing but regret.

UROOJ SYED

Beauty

Beauty is in the eye of the beholder. This graphite pencil drawing depicts admiration for beauty and love.

JORDAN CURRIE

Condolence Party

Funeral homes always fittingly seemed to smell like death.

Simultaneously of dust and something clean, too clean, as if the entire premises had been rubbed raw with cleaning solution. The funerals Darla attended when she was a kid had that same lingering smell, the same horrid 70s floral print on the worn carpets and deflated cushioned chairs, the same triangular cold cut sandwiches, the same sallow faces.

This one was no exception. Darla shifts uncomfortably in the musty arm chair in the lobby of the funeral home. She's wearing the only dress she owns, a shapeless black thing she got when she was 13, a time when she was expected to wear such things growing into adolescence. It doesn't fit her now and it didn't when she was 13. That's what her mother gets for letting her pick it out herself— nothing like what she wanted her daughter to look like, but instead potato sack chic. She's developed some affection for the ugly thing.

She watches her family from where they're spread across the room like black bugs, part scattered about and part huddled together in mini groups. Cliques and social hierarchy, as all families had but no one dared to admit.

Darla walks up to her grandmother, crying and signing a guest book with a melodramatic message and her signature. She pulls a handkerchief out of her breast pocket and dabs at the faint stream of tears, almost non-existent to the human eye.

"Tragedy, isn't it?" Darla says. Her grandmother continues sniffling.

"There there, Meryl," Darla tells her. "It'll get better in time. Crying isn't a good look for you."

She leaves when her grandmother doesn't respond in favour of crying into the raggedy handkerchief. Her other family members look similar—all nodding along to whatever story was being told or shaking their heads in mock disbelief. Perhaps Darla isn't being totally fair—some form of grief is always present in the atmosphere when someone dies. But she has some understanding of how these people operate. They cry plastic tears. Darla wants to puke.

Her mother Sarah is glued to her cell phone, sending strong "don't bother me" signals to everyone in the room with her hunched posture and stoic face. Her tears seem to have dried up for the time being, but Darla knows her mother is capable of turning on that faucet whenever she wants to. Darla stands directly in front of her, wanting to say something but also not, knowing there's no use when it comes to Sarah.

Darla wanders around, eavesdropping on various conversations happening between her family members and the seldom friends that showed up. They're all filled with *I'm sorry* and *how terrible* and *she was my best friend, we did everything together* and *she's in a better place* and *oh my god what are you doing this weekend? We should go shoe shopping, mine are getting so worn out.* Darla shrugs. You can't expect everyone to be so sad all the fucking time.

There's people at this funeral that Darla's never even met before, yet they all have such kind things to say. It's overwhelming, really. She often fanaticized about her own death when she was little. How many people would show up to the funeral, who would cry the most, what people would say in their eulogies, what kind of food would be served. Although, probably nothing spectacular. Most likely egg salad sandwiches and stale cookies and lukewarm coffee. It was always the same at every funeral. Same went for the eulogies.

"She was an incredible young lady," says a voice from behind her. She turns around and a nameless man is hugging her aunt. "She's in a better place."

Darla almost laughs out loud. "You're lucky to be so sure," she mutters.

Bored of the tear fest, Darla makes her way into the viewing room where nobody is allowed inside yet, but she manages to slip past the door without anyone noticing anyway. The casket rests at the far opposite end of the room. She walks toward it, legs feeling like she's moving through honey, remembering when Meryl cried just as hard when Darla shaved her head, or when Sarah looked just as stone cold when she threw a glass bottle across the room after she walked in on her kissing Lucy in her room that one summer evening, or how I love you's were like leap year in her house, or how she didn't know the people outside and they didn't know her and they were crying, crying, crying.

The casket is half open, bouquets of white lilies flooding the space around to mask the smell of formaldehyde. Darla stares down into it and sees her own face not staring back up at her because the body in the casket is dead and can't do anything anymore. The hands are folded neatly across the abdomen. Someone had painted the fingernails a soft blush pink colour. She looks at her own fingernails, the ones she has now, permanently, short and unkempt.

"You were always sort of dead to them," she says to the body. She looks longingly at the corpse, picturing a life they could have had, with or without her ghost family for a fraction of a moment before sighing and stepping away from the casket.

"My condolences," she says, her voice drowned by the silence of the room.

NISHKA GUPTA

At The Age Of

At the age of 5 everything was okay,
I could wear shorts and dresses,
And my Mother would say,
Wow you look beautiful each and every day,
But now since I have grown,
Everything that I have known,
Isn't the truth anymore?

At the age of 7, I was a princess,
My favourite colour was pink before I could even think,
I wanted to put on tutus and do ballet,
It all seems so cliché,
The reason that I didn't play sports,
Was because I was taught that girls could not own the court,
We played princess while the boys played basketball,
They played soccer while I played with my Barbie dolls,
How can this be fair?

At the age of 12, I learned about toxicity in life,
I learned about how words can cut just like a knife,
I was too scared to stand up to anybody at that time,
Because me being a girl getting off of my seat is a crime,
Words were bashing me every day,
Like stupid, ugly, and they just stayed,
They pierced into my skin because I am a female,
Who was too scared to fight back because I was not a free male?

At the age of 14 everything changed,
It all was so strange,
I couldn't wear a short dress,
Because my Father would stress.
I wasn't allowed to go walk to the park,
Let alone step out of my house in the dark,

Because my sister is too afraid to let me go out at all,
She is scared that I may get cat called,
But it's not my fault that the world is like this,
That men just want to hiss,
At girls.

At the age of 15, it has got worse,
There should be an end put to this curse,
It isn't okay to touch girls without permission,
We don't give out free tickets so you can have admission,
We aren't a magician to show you tricks,
So just leave us alone and don't call us chicks.

At the age of 16 I learned,
I learned that women do not deserve to be verbally burned,
I learned that women can play sports and prevail,
I learned that women are not for sale,
I learned that I have a voice,
I learned that women have a choice,
I learned that women have to stick together,
Together as feminists.

JACKI SHI

Ego Vs. Self

Embracing duality.

PUJITA VERMA

De-Titled

I have never learned how to fold a memory
Into origami ornaments meant for
back pockets instead of showcases
To treasure paper treasures the way we do
meaningful accessories

The way we can't seem to forget what
We needed to remember
And can't seem to remember what
We never intended to forget
To learn that folded memories still told stories,
No matter what form they took.

Sometimes we told these stories with fading letters on tainted
    pages
Or in withering journals and one-way conversations and
In between the chords,
Sometimes we tell them in songs
Or twice (not half)—hearted paint brush strokes
Other times we tell them on sidewalks in small, meaningful
exchanges; because a story is a story
No matter how we tell it.

Though meaning can be lost in translation.
Like how language can hold us together
But keep us divided
Like how we sometimes can't find the word to describe
the feeling, the moment, the loss or the joy

Or the way the sun swallowed the hospital waiting room
on the day I held my sister for the first time and knew
she would become the reason I believed in miracles

The way we all have our reasons
The way we are always trying to find the words to say

Maybe we lose ourselves in commotion
But find each other in the connotations
As every moment is worthy of becoming a sidewalk story
Maybe not everyone will comprehend your back pocket origami
    memory
But we all have something to say
Even if you can't find the right word

You can phrase it in a metaphor
You make the language for your storytelling
Everyone else finds their way in understanding
And you find your way
In **telling your story**

SEREEN AZIZ

Refugees at Sea

PRASIDDHA PARTHASARATHY

Cameo

"**Sonder** *n.* the realization that each random passerby is living a
life as vivid and complex as your own."
—John Koenig, *The Dictionary of Obscure Sorrows*

Dear World,

Is it not enthralling that every smile uncovers a tale, a legend?
That grimaces hide waterfalls, wrinkles betray past and present?
To every soul I have the honour of meeting,
I thank you for the moments we share, even if fleeting.
For they let me peer inside, take a glimpse at a part of you.
Though you may be a minor role in my life's play, you have
    played a part, and that is irrevocably true!

For that moment where we meet, I can't see the number of likes
    you have,
Or the countless memes in which you've been tagged!
Your name too remains unknown, but for that one moment in
    life,
We are human, and a stitch in time we have sown.

I glance around me on the bus, my curious eyes silently
    wandering.
To the baby with the shiny eyes, a high-fashion icon,
all-conquering.
To the girl with her earphones on, bobbing her head in
    harmony,
To the bus driver thanking each passenger upon entry, a subtle,
    endearing philanthropy.

Before my stop arrives, I play a game in my mind.
Weaving together backstories is my pastime, one of its kind.
Is she a Jane Austen lover, preferring a book by the fireplace on
    a Friday night?
Or he a piano prodigy, fingers worn and riddled with insight?
Is the bus driver a polyglot, speaking one tongue among seven?
Or that baby destined for greatness, a superstar by profession?

The greatest question of all,
is that you too may be wondering the same.
Who am I, and what is my name?
The prospects of human connection
are both bountiful and thrilling,
So though in this moment, we bid farewell, thank you for
    cameo'ing in my life—you have made it most fulfilling. :)

Youth Support Services and Organizations

Our Place Peel

If you're 16 to 21 and have nowhere to go, Our Place Peel can help. At the Emergency Shelter in Mississauga, you'll find safe shelter, a warm bed, and a hot meal waiting for you any time of the day or night.

www.ourplacepeel.org | 3579 Dixie Rd, Mississauga | (905) 238-1383

The Dam

The Dam (Develop, Assist, Mentor) is a community non-profit that supports youth-at-risk, by providing a drop-in where youth are free to hang out.

www.thedam.org | 6850 Millcreek Dr., Mississauga | (905) 826-6558

Tangerine Walk-In Counselling

Tangerine Walk-In Counselling is available free of charge to children and youth, and their parents, caregivers or adult supporters. Adolescents aged 12 to 17 may access this service independently.

www.tangerinewalkin.com | (905) 795-3530 | Multiple Locations

Nexus Youth Services

Since 1984, Nexus Youth Services has offered counselling services to teenagers and young adults like you, ages 14 to 24, who live in the Region of Peel in Ontario, Canada.

nexusyouth.ca | 85A Aventura Court, Mississauga | (905) 566-1883
24/7 Crisis Line: 416-410-8615 (under 18); 905-278-9036 (over 18)

Kids Help Phone

Kids Help Phone is Canada's only bilingual phone and on-line counselling service for youth. It's free, anonymous and confidential. Professional counsellors are available any time of the day or night, 365 days a year, to help young people deal with concerns large or small.

www.kidshelpphone.ca | 1-800-668-6868

Art Gallery of Mississauga and Ink Movement:

Border Crossings

Borders are both physical places, marked by barriers in the form of walls or coasts, and imaginary ones, indicated only by lines on a map, or places in our hearts. They are paradoxical, in that they both connect and divide. But they are, first and foremost, stories. Stories of changes in perspective—physical, psychological and ideological. Border —a community engagement lab is archeology of the present and uses stories and narratives to fuel an alternative means of seeing across a broad range of physical and cultural contexts. Border Crossings is a participative, inclusive 'art and story' experience designed for communities to reflect, co-create, and share.

For seven weeks visitors to the gallery and workshop participants were invited to use the different stations in the gallery to share their stories and experiences with crossing borders— geographical, linguistic, spiritual and personal. What a mosaic of stories they left behind.

~ *Sharada K Eswar*

Community Activator, Art Gallery of Mississauga

I'm of
the diversity
RESPECT
love

home

BORDER CROSSINGS

I grew up knowing that borders would separate my family because my father had to work in Canada, and we would stay somewhere else

I knew that we would join him soon, but borders were something that were difficult to overcome, that they were vast oceans and time differences and weak phone connections.

I grew up with my own borders drawn by the people around me that outlined the person I would grow up to be.

I grew up thinking I was defined as a daughter, a sister, a future wife and mother, forever a connection to someone else.

I grew up with the idea that there was already a dotted line set out in front of me, and all I needed to do was follow.

But, when we finally flew over the oceans and clouds that separated my family, the world widened and borders were smudged.

Years later, I know that the borders others drew for me were lined in chalk and I can erase them and make my own.

I know that I am more than someone else's ______.

I know that I will always have my own chalk and my own eraser to change whatever borders I want.

I know now that I can step outside the circle drawn years ago by others, that my life is my own.

I know that I will make mistakes but they will be my own.

I am not defined by any borders and I will grow to learn and continue to step over the lines holding me back.

Artists

Aaron Chua
Grade 12

Abeera Shahid
Age 20
McMaster University

Adriano Brown
Age 18

Aiken Yong
Age 20
York University

Aiman Faheem
Age 18
Independent Learning Centre

Ali Malik
Age 16
White Oaks Secondary School

Amanda Joy Ceballos Lopos
Age 14
St. Joan of Arc Catholic
Secondary School

Amira Bouchema
Age 16
St Joan of Arc Catholic
Secondary School

Ananya Ananth
Age 17
Glenforest Secondary School

Angela He
Age 16
St. Francis Xavier Secondary
School

Anisha Mehra
Age 16
Rick Hansen Secondary School

Areeb Athar
Age 17
White Oaks Secondary School

Ayana Siddiqui
Glenforest Secondary School

Carol Markos
Age 19
McMaster University

Charu Sharma
Age 18
University of Western Ontario

Dana-Kaye Matthews
Age 18
University of Ottawa

Daniella Serrador
Age 17
Port Credit Secondary School

Deeksha Chaudhery
Age 16
Harold M. Brathwaite

Dhanbir Singh Thethi
Age 17
Louise Arbour Secondary School

Doaa Shaikh
Age 24
University of Toronto

Emily McDowell
Age 19
Humber college

Fiona Yang
Age 16

Geraldine Svic
Age 21
OCAD University

Hailey Tsolakis
Age 20
Sheridan College

Heba Alfayez
Age 15
Rick Hansen Secondary School

Jacki Shi
Age 17
White Oaks

Jaylon Pascual
Age 16
St Joan of Arc

Jordan Currie
Age 20
Ryerson University

Justina Yang
Age 17
White Oaks Secondary School

Kaneera Uthayakumaran
Age 14
Tomken Road Middle School

Kay Wu
Age 18
Queen's University

Keeva Szeto
Age 16
Rick Hansen Secondary School

Kelly Estomo
Age 20
York University

Kenisha Arora
Age 15
Glenforest Secondary School

Khyathi Rao
Age 15
Glenforest Secondary School

Kirollos Kilada
Age 19
OCAD University

Komal Patel
Age 19
Western University

Lucy Zhang
Age 17
White Oaks Secondary School

Marium Khan
Age 14
Bishop Reding Catholic
Secondary School

Matt Lau
Age 16
Rick Hansen Secondary School

Melanie Klingel
Age 17
Glenforest Secondary School

Melissa Rezk
Age 19
Wilfrid Laurier University

Miho Nagayama
Age 18
University of Waterloo

Nishka Gupta
Age 16
Central peel Secondary School

Noor B. Toeama
Age 16
Dr. Frank J. Hayden Secondary
School

Prasiddha Parthasarathy
Age 19
McMaster University

Pujita Verma
Age 17
Glenforest Secondary School

Rianna Alarakhia
Age 15
John Fraser Secondary School

Sadia Sheikh
Age 21
Ryerson University

Saleha Ansari
Age 17
Glenforest Secondary School

Sally Co
Age 18
Rick Hansen Secondary School

Sanaz Bani
Age 16
Rick Hansen Secondary School

Seerat Rehman
Age 17
Rick Hansen Secondary School

Selena Zhou
Age 14
Tomken Road Middle School

Sereen Aziz
Age 17
White Oaks Secondary School

Shoffana Sundaramoorthy
Age 16
Central Peel Secondary School

Steven Cheung
Age 17
Cawthra Park SS

Surutiga Ranjan
Age 17
St. Francis Xavier Secondary
School

Urooj Syed
Age 19
University of Toronto

Vaishnavy Gangadaran
Age 17
Glenforest Secondary School

Valentina Caballero
Age 19
Ryerson University

Veronica Montecalvo
Age 17
John Cabot Catholic Secondary
School

Warwick Pang
Age 17
Glenforest Secondary School

William
Age 17
Stephen Lewis Secondary School
(Vaughan)

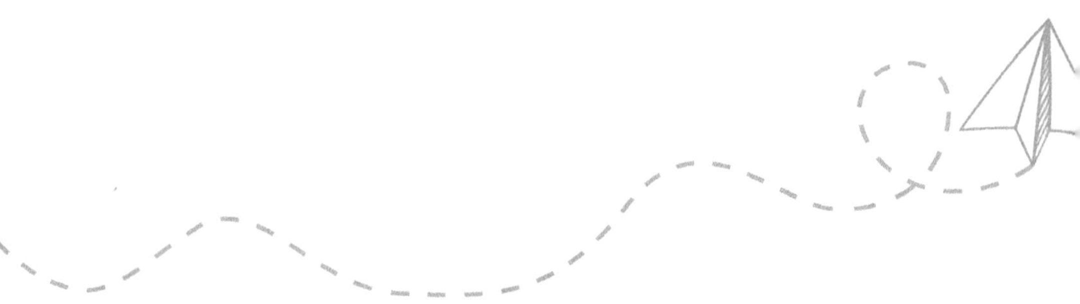

Acknowledgments

The Mississauga Youth Anthology: Volume VI would not have been possible without the contributions of our generous community partners and dedicated Ink Movement family!

Thank you to the Ontario Ministry of Education for generously supporting this year's project through the Student Voice Speak-Up Grants; to the City of Mississauga for your dedication to promoting Ink Movement's goals through funding and support; to the Art Gallery of Mississauga for their continuous support through Ink Movement's initiatives; to Cheryl Antao-Xavier and her team at In Our Words Inc. for publishing the Anthology; and finally, thank you to our community supporters for making the Anthology a great success!

Thank you to this year's extraordinary Ink Movement 2017-2018 team: Amna Zia, Pujita Verma, Zijian Zhang, Tahira Alarakhia, Khyathi Rao, Tanmay Deotale, Lyba Fatima, Emi Roni, Aleeza Qayyum, Seerat Rehman, Catherine Hu, Sally Co, Maham Momin, Cecilia Tsang, Adrian Aliu, Brian Sun, Waris Zahoor, Jacki Shi, Muhammad Usman Ghani, Steven Van, Arav Dagli, Fiona Yang, John Miranda, Hunnain Atif, Kiran Bassi, Nishka Gupta, Ayana Siddiqui, Saher Shergill, Elliot Lam, Isra Amsdr, and Abi Sudharshan

Once again, I'd like to thank our editors—Emi Roni, Aleeza Qayyum, Seerat Rehman, Catherine Hu, and Sally Co for their time and dedication to brainstorming and editing the Anthology, and our talented graphic designers—Sally Co, Cecilia Tsang and Adrian Aliu for the incredible promotional material and cover designs. You were a truly special team. Finally, thank you to Maxwell Tran for his extended support throughout the entire process and for creating an outlet of self-expression for the amazing and talented youth in our community.

Sincerely,

Rana Al-Fayez, Anthology Lead

Sonya Zhang, President